SEVEN SINS

MIGUEL ESTRADA

Copyright © 2020 Miguel Estrada.

All rights reserved.

This is a work of fiction. Names, characters, places and incidents are used in a fictitious manner. Any resemblance to actual events, or persons, living or dead, is coincidental. No part of this publication may be reproduced, or transmitted in any form or by any means, electronic or otherwise, without written permission from the author.

WARNING: This book contains scenes of violence and disturbing themes. Please enjoy at your own discretion.

TABLE OF CONTENTS

Greed 1

Gluttony 7

Wrath 10

Pride 14

Sloth 19

Lust 23

Greed 31

Sloth 35

Pride 42

Greed 49

Lust 58

Pride 66

Gluttony 72

Lust 76

Sloth 85

Gluttony 88

Wrath 92

Pride 95

Wrath 102

Sloth 109

Gluttony 116

Pride 120

Lust 124

Sloth 130

Pride 137

Wrath 140

Greed 144

Gluttony 148

Lust 151

Sloth 155

Pride 158

Gluttony 162

Wrath 166

Greed 168

Lust 172

Sloth 178

Envy 187

Lust 191

Greed 196

Sloth 200

Lust 204

Sloth 209

Greed 218

Sloth 225

Lust 232

Sloth 238

Lust 245

Sloth 249

Jessica 258

Would You Like To Leave A Review? 263

GREED

The house Roger was looking for stood at the end of a blind street, away from all the others. The job should be easier than usual. Roger reached into the pockets of his jacket and put on his gloves. He raised the black hoodie over his head while taking one last glance over his shoulder before continuing.

The faint orange glow of the lampposts illuminated the path before him. The neighborhood was desolate. The bare tree branches rustling with the wind were the only sound to be heard from miles away.

Roger eyed his watch. It was 11:32 p.m. The house's residents were probably boarding their flight by now. Roger had studied them carefully. While the family of four lived humbly, they had inherited a fortune in collectibles that they still kept in the house.

By the time they returned from their vacation, however, Roger would have sold everything.

The lock of the main entrance lock was standard, just a tiny inconvenience for someone with a bit of talent and the right tools. Entering a house was not the challenge; it had never been for him.

The burglary business was a very lucrative one and one in which Roger had become very efficient. The problem was another.

The dog.

An eighty-pound, black pit bull had been left behind as guardian of the house—a dragon protecting its treasure, as some may say. Roger had considered that and came prepared. A slice of raw meat with sleeping pills should suffice to do the trick. If it didn't, then he'd have to improvise, and improvising wasn't his forte.

Roger sighed. He had heard how vicious that breed could be. While there were people who argued that pit bulls were no different than any other dog breeds regarding aggressiveness or jaw strength, it wasn't something that Roger was eager to find out.

Roger now stood a few feet away from the residence. Then, as if summoned, the dog promptly started barking from behind the wooden fence, loud and clear. Definitely not the warning kind of bark.

Roger slipped the slice of raw steak out of his jacket and threw it over the fence. The barking ceased. Roger approached the fence on the tip of his toes, leaning closer and peeping through the cracks. The dog seemed to be enjoying the meal.

With no more time to spare, Roger circled the house and waited for a minute or two. The cold air of the night was welcoming, and Roger had learned to associate it with a job well done. To think how much he would make from one score made him crack a smile. Eager, he jumped over the fence and strode to the back door. His lock-picking skills were no match for an ordinary back door.

Once inside, Roger found himself embraced by the darkness of the residence. Leaving the dog behind made him feel safer, as he could finally breathe easy, if only for a second, before continuing with his mission. He pulled out his flashlight and scanned the place. The kitchen seemed conventional, if not a bit dull, not the kind of place where they'd keep valuables. The collection would probably be in the attic or the basement. Perhaps, it would be locked inside a safe—piece of cake.

Roger crept to the living room, internalizing everything around him. *The Devil's in the details*, as his father used to say. However, his father probably never imagined that his son would follow his advice in this manner. Robbing houses wasn't something Roger was exactly proud of, but it brought bread to the table.

What would my old man think if he saw me like this? Given the circumstances, I think he'd understand. At least, I hope so.

Roger shook those thoughts out of his head and decided to focus on his task. Worrying about the opinion of someone who had been dead for over fifteen years wasn't going to get him anywhere.

One of the doors to his right stood ajar. He pushed it gently, the hinges squeaking. At his feet, a set of stairs led down. Maybe it was better to check the basement first and go up from there. Roger marched down, his footsteps echoing in the dark. A spectral figure in the corner of his eye made him stop dead in his tracks. He felt his heart skip a beat as he pointed the flashlight toward the shadow.

It was a coat hanging from the wall.

Roger let out a sigh of relief. He had never been the scaredy-cat type. If he were, he would have a hard time in the business of barging into empty houses in the middle of the night. Still, there wasn't such a thing as being too careful.

Roger inspected every nook and cranny of the large basement. It took way longer than he'd expected, but just when he was about to call it a day, he noticed a segment of bricks in the wall that was a little less moldy than the others around it.

Bingo.

He inserted his fingers between the fissures of the bricks. He placed the flashlight on his mouth as he groped his belt to get a couple of tools. With a screwdriver serving as a makeshift lever, he pulled out several bricks, revealing a safe hidden inside the wall. However, this one was different from the ones he was used to cracking. Usually, he could easily outwit the safes where he could rotate the numbers. But this one was a digital safe, with a keypad and a screen that illuminated faint, green numbers.

Great, now I need to figure out the password. This is going to be a pain in the ass.

Roger shrugged. The job was only going to take a little longer than expected, that was all. He could inspect the rest of the house for clues. From experience, he knew that most people's passwords were hidden in plain sight. Only a keen eye and a bit of brainpower were needed—a birthday marked on the calendar, an anniversary, a phone number. However, before he could even begin his search, a chilling noise, like that of claws scraping through wood accompanied by an ominous growl, made the hairs of his body stand on end.

Roger stayed put for a second, trying to figure out what the hell had happened. He was sure the dog had eaten the meat.

He swallowed dry, scanning the place for something to defend himself, a bat or a golf club, anything. He didn't like the idea of having to hurt a dog, but if his other option was to be bitten by jaws as strong as those of a shark, then he had no choice. Roger wished that what he had read on the Internet about pit bulls wasn't true.

A silvery hint of light blinked from the corner of his eye. He turned to see an aluminum bat leaning against the brick wall on the other side of the room. A glint of hope grew inside him. Roger lunged toward the bat and grabbed it like his life depended on it. With his heart in his throat, Roger climbed back up the stairs.

The only thing he could hear besides his own breathing was the ticking of a clock somewhere, a maddening sound that had him clenching his jaw. Then a subtle growl from right behind him.

Roger spun around, hoping to find the pit bull that had given him a not-so-warm welcome. But, to his surprise, it was a Rottweiler. The hound displayed a row of white fangs and a thread of saliva reaching the ground.

What's wrong with these people? Don't they have two children?

Before he could follow his train of thought, the dog charged at full speed toward him. Roger tried to throw a swing at the dog, but instead, he instinctively raised the bat to his face horizontally. The Rottweiler jumped, opening its jaws in the air.

The dog's fangs bit the bat's body, biting desperately and trying to dig into the metal. Roger's back slammed against the ground. The man and the beast struggled as the animal's saliva soaked Roger's face. The Rottweiler's eyes burned with hatred. Despite the beast's incredible strength, Roger managed to place his feet on the dog's ribs and kick it back.

The dog let out a howl when it hit the wall. Roger sprang up in less than a second and dashed toward the house entrance, pushing the door open with all the weight of his body. The pit bull slept peacefully in the courtyard next to the piece of meat that had only a couple of bites left to finish. Roger climbed the fence with a single leap and fell on the other side. There was a tearing sound, and Roger felt the Rottweiler's teeth scraping over his leg, almost biting him.

Roger looked down to see his pants ripped, his heart beating fast, and his lungs gasping desperately for air.

The dog repeatedly jumped, trying to poke his head over the fence while barking his lungs out. Finally, Roger shook off his clothes and hurried back to where he had come from.

I'm sorry, ma. I let you down...

GLUTTONY

Matthew let the cold water run between his fingers, carrying the soft layer of soap on his skin. He grabbed the knife on the counter and began cutting the vegetables with expertise. Cooking was his passion; it always had been. Even now, after getting home from a long day's work, the only thing that relaxed him was to put on his apron and prepare the meals for the week.

Matt grabbed the veggies and skimmed them with the knife toward the pan. The hissing sound of oil drew a smile on his face. His reflection in the knife made him pause a moment. It had always seemed somewhat poetic to see himself on the edge of the metal. His other self returned his gaze, calm as the sea, with a brown beard and a completely bald head. His face, even when he was stern, seemed upbeat and welcoming. The irony was not lost on him.

The doorbell pulled him out of his trance. Who could it be at this hour? Matthew wiped his hands and strode to the entrance. He peeked through the door's magic eye. A big-nosed lady not taller than 5'2" stood patiently at the other side.

Of course, it's Regina. Who else could've been?

Matt took a deep breath, changed the cold expression on his face to a friendlier one, and opened the door.

"Hey, Regina! How is it going?"

"Matty!" The lady beamed. "How are you, my darling? I hope I'm not interrupting anything."

"Actually . . ."

Before she could proceed, the tiny lady stepped in and entered the residence, her fly eyes scanning everything around her. "I've been waiting for you all day. I didn't know you'd leave the hospital so late."

"Actually, I offered to stay a little longer." *I didn't want to deal with anyone else today.*

"Oh, that's so kind of you," Mrs. Regina said. "Always giving to people who need it. The world should be full of men like you, Matty, definitely. Today I was thinking about that how there can be people like you who give and give and ask for nothing in return. So I decided to bring this to you." The lady reached into her massive purse, which was almost the size of her whole torso, and pulled out a circular package covered in aluminum. Considering the shape and the smell, it had to be one of her homemade cakes. "It's an old family recipe."

The lady circled Matt and walked straight to the kitchen. Matthew's heart skipped a beat. He jumped toward the fridge and leaned against it. Regina's head jerked back in surprise.

"Excuse me, Mrs. Regina," said Matt. "It's just that I haven't cleaned the fridge in a while. It's a mess, and I'd hate it if you saw it like that."

The lady cocked an eyebrow but then shrugged. "Well, no problem, honey. I'll leave it here." Regina placed the cake on the dining room bar that separated the kitchen from the living room. "What are you cooking? Lamb? It smells delicious."

"Uh, yes, lamb."

"Well, I'll leave you alone then. Sorry if I bothered you."

"Oh, no, not at all, Mrs. Regina. I apologize. You just caught me off guard. Had I known you were coming, I would've cleaned and made dinner sooner."

She smiled. "I'll call next time, dear. Ciao ciao."

The tiny woman left and disappeared into the night. Matt let out a sigh as he locked the door. He went back to the kitchen and opened the fridge, immensely relieved to have arrived on time before his nosy neighbor had a chance to see inside.

Wrapped in plastic was a severed human hand, still fresh, with contorted fingers toward the center as if trying to make a fist. Matthew was thankful for putting it in the fridge to defrost it instead of leaving it in the sink.

It was a close call.

Matthew took the severed hand, put it on the table, and continued to prepare his plate. It was going to be exquisite.

WRATH

Trevor drank the last sip of his bourbon. The bar's music was eclipsed by other customers' conversations around him and the game playing on the television. The world had begun to spin five glasses ago, but the pain had not dimmed in the slightest. It never did. It was only when his body couldn't even stand anymore that Trevor knew something similar to peace, and he still had a few more drinks to get to that point.

"Johnny!" he called. "Another! Straight-up!"

The bartender approached, looked at Trevor from top to bottom, and shrugged. Trevor watched as the sinful liquid filled the glass and wished the glasses were larger. All sounds around him began to disappear, to blur into each other until they were nothing more than background noise. Suddenly, the laughter of a girl in his ears made him relax. All the muscles in his body released tension as if a huge weight had been lifted from his shoulders. The hairs on his right arm bristled, a current of electricity running through his skin, simulating the delicate touch of a woman. Trevor looked down to his arm but saw nothing, no one at his side. Neither the girl nor the woman.

The screeching of wheels on pavement brought him out of his trance. Trevor jumped up, his lost gaze circling around him. His eyes darted to the window behind him. Through the neon lights, he could make out the street outside. There were no cars.

Inside the bar, however, there were several people whose conversations had suddenly stopped. Everyone was staring at him. Trevor felt the blood rise to his cheeks. A familiar warmth passed through his chest like a flame inside him.

"The fuck are ya'll looking at?" he barked before taking a seat again and finishing the drink. "Another!"

This time, the bartender shot him a glance and looked elsewhere. That son of a bitch was ignoring him. An asshole sitting next to Trevor muttered something under his breath.

"What the fuck did you say, bitch?" Trevor challenged. He wasn't going to take anyone's shit. "Say it to my face."

The asshole, who was six foot five, turned over his shoulder with irritating serenity.

"I said that you should shut your mouth," said the giant as he stood up.

Trevor didn't feel intimidated in the slightest. He was used to sweep the floor with people of that caliber, huge gorillas who believed they could walk over others because of their size. If there was something he had learned while in the army, it was that size did not mean much, especially if they were on the other side of a gun. Everyone had the same weaknesses, and they bled the same way.

"You have balls, big guy," Trevor said, stepping forward. "I can make you eat them for lunch."

Johnny now focused his attention on Trevor; he had left the area behind the bar and put a hand on Trevor's shoulder. "Hey, T, leave it. It is not worth making a scene."

"I'm not making a scene," Trevor shot, his eyes piercing the bartender's skull. "This wannabe princess is the one making a fuss."

The giant threw a punch in his direction. Trevor received the hit straight to the chin. Trevor's neck turned sharply, and a red thread made an arc in the air from his upper lip to the ground. Trevor managed to keep his balance. A throbbing pain embraced the left side of his face. He cracked his knuckles and wiped his lip with his forearm.

The giant in front of him stood tall like a building. The giant's face turned from surprise to confusion as if he couldn't believe that Trevor had withstood such a blow. The former soldier had endured much worse.

"You call that a swing, princess?" Trevor mocked.

There were laughs. A group of spectators gathered around them. The giant prepared to deliver the next punch, putting his weight on one foot, but Trevor was faster. Two clean strikes. One in the right rib and one in the eye. Trevor's body reacted instinctively despite his drunken state, in which he had begun to see the bar around him spinning. The giant's head jerked back with the second blow, and then the rest of his body followed him to the ground. The wooden floor shook at the impact of such a behemoth.

Trevor cracked his neck, ready to leave the matter settled. He turned and reached into his pocket to pay for his tab. However, a collective gasp made him stop. Trevor watched the giant stand up again, ready for another round.

This one is not as soft as I thought.

The man lunged at Trevor. Trevor quickly grabbed one of the bottles on the counter and smashed it into the giant's face. Thousands of tiny glass shards flew in all directions. The man fell on top of the counter, knocking out bottles and glasses. After that, his huge body slid and returned to the ground.

"Enough!" The bartender shouted. "I will call the police! I'm not having any of this shit in my bar!"

"Call whoever you want," Trevor spat. "I'm outta here."

"You're not going anywhere, Trevor!" Johnny threatened.

"If you don't want to end up like that asshole, don't tell me what to do."

Trevor stormed out of the bar.

PRIDE

Timothy Wilson, business magnate, CEO of his own company, husband and father of two, a girl and a boy, could not ask for more out of life. He was surrounded by people who either admired him or licked his boots. And after all the years of effort, he knew the importance of recognizing the difference between the two. One group only tossed compliments at him, expecting praise or a promotion, while the other asked for legitimate advice and imitated his behavior. The second group was gold, always.

Timothy put his arm around the shoulder of his beautiful wife, Linda, a tall woman with light green eyes and flawless black hair that fell like a waterfall to her glutes. The two presented a bright smile for the cameras.

The courtyard of the Saint-Mary hospital was flooded with people. Hospital staff, a few reporters, and dozens of children, some in wheelchairs, others in brakes, all with some type of disability. The local news had arrived an hour before the event began in order to set up the equipment, fix up cables, and rehearse. Tim assumed that not much was happening in the small town he had grown up in for the news to cover such a small charity event.

Timothy had been the main contributor to that event, donating just under eighty percent of what was collected, so it was no wonder why the public's attention was entirely focused on him. He had always had a weak point for the disabled. His brother was born with cerebral palsy. Tim had spent much of his childhood taking care of his baby brother well into his twenties. It was then that complications took the life of his younger sibling, so Timothy had taken upon himself the mission to care for the needs of both his mother and father. Ten years later, Timothy Wilson had become a millionaire. Now his father and mother lived in a mansion on the outskirts of the city, with everything they could ever need so that they did not have to worry about anything else or go through any efforts for the rest of their lives.

Even so, Tim never stopped grieving the loss of his brother. And now, he had been presented with the opportunity to change the life, not of one, but of dozens of children whose parents could not afford expensive treatments and lacked the requirements to have decent insurance. Tim kissed his wife's forehead and ruffled his son's hair, who was standing next to his sister. Tim struggled to remember the last time the kids had spent that amount of time together without fighting.

Tim stepped into the podium with dozens of eyes fixed on him. He was used to the attention, but that did not stop his stomach from showing a small hit of nervousness.

Tim cleared his throat and recited the speech he had prepared the night before. When he finished, he received a hail of applause. He could see in the public how there were parents like him, wiping away the tears of happiness, for the opportunity to have a little hope. Tim felt his heart fill with warmth.

As soon as he stepped down from the podium, Tim received a hug from his wife and a kiss on the cheek. At that time, public displays of affection were more courtesy than genuine. While their domestic life was peaceful and they had nothing to envy of most couples, they had been married for more than thirteen years, which can have the effect of making things a little . . . monotonous. The flame of passion that had united them during their relationship and the first years of marriage had gradually vanished, like a campfire at the mercy of the cold wind of the night.

Tim suspected they were together more out of habit than anything else, that and fear of change so late in the game. There were also the children, who were barely eight and ten years old. Even so, despite the monotony, Tim could not imagine a life with someone other than her and his children.

The flash of the cameras started to die down until, finally, people began to lose interest, giving room for the people he truly cared about: the children and their parents. Some shook hands with tears in their eyes; others hugged them, full of gratitude. But the one who would become embedded into his mind like no other was a lady in her fifties, short stature, chubby figure, and tanned skin. The woman was pushing a young man in a wheelchair. The boy couldn't be older than twenty years old. The chair carried an oxygen tank attached to the side. The boy, however, did not have the mask on. The tank was most likely a preventive measure in case the young man had trouble breathing.

The boy's pale skin reflected the morning sun and his eyes, covered by dark circles and filled with the fatigue of an old man, still reflected a special glow as a smile grew on his face. The woman, who had to be the child's mother, threw herself at Tim with open arms.

He had to make an effort not to be pushed back. The woman was considerably strong despite her size.

"Oh, thank you very much, Mr. Wilson," the lady said. She had a slight Hispanic accent.

"You have nothing to thank for," he replied. "It's my pleasure to help you." His gaze fixed on the boy. Despite having a weak frame and being so thin that the skin seemed to adhere to his bones, Tim perceived strength in the young fellow, a determination in his eyes that he had only seen in his own brother so many years ago. He was tempted to ask about his situation but figured that kind of question might be inappropriate.

"He has paraplegia," said the lady as if she had read his mind. "He lost most of the function of his body after we nearly lost him to a car accident. It's such a blessing that you created this program. I had no idea how I was gonna afford the treatment for my little boy." The lady was on the verge of tears, her face contorted in an effort not to get carried away by emotion.

"Well, you have nothing to worry about. Very soon, he will have the treatment and care he deserves."

The woman could not take it anymore. Tears flooded out and slid down her face like a fountain. She gave Tim a second hug. She lowered her voice to a whisper that only Tim could hear. "The doctors didn't give him much time. They said it was a miracle he was even alive."

Tim pushed her gently away, his tone equally low. "God has a plan for him. He's still alive because he has a lot to give. So, keep your chin up and don't lose hope."

The woman nodded and buried her face in Tim's arms one last time. When she separated from him, Tim approached the boy in the wheelchair. He bent on one knee and leaned down to eye level.

"You are strong, young man. Don't let anyone tell you otherwise."

"I'm sorry he's quiet," the lady said. "He lost his speech over time, but that doesn't stop him from being the smartest person in the house."

Tim beamed a smile. "I'm sure he is."

The woman said her goodbyes. The young man simply smiled and raised his palm a little. Tim assumed that was as much as the boy could do. He returned the gesture and walked away.

Timothy glanced around the courtyard to where his children were. They were running, chasing each other throughout the place, probably playing tag or something. Tim thanked God. He felt incredibly lucky that he not only had everything he'd ever wanted, but he also had the opportunity to give back. A smile grew on his face as he watched his children play.

That day deserved a celebration.

SLOTH

Oliver took a deep puff of his joint. Smoke filled his lungs, and a familiar burning feeling flooded his chest. He let the smoke out through his mouth and nostrils. In a few minutes, the ceiling of the room was almost completely covered by a faint white layer of mist. Oliver felt his muscles relax; his legs were so light that he felt they would float away without him. He was content.

A horrendous tune startled him out of his trance. His phone was ringing. The name Aunt Ana was displayed on the screen. Oliver rubbed his face with one hand before answering. The only reason his aunt called him was to scold him or ask for a favor. He held the phone in his hand for several seconds while considering what to do. It took him a moment to realize that he had to press the green button to answer.

"Hello?" he said hoarsely.

"Hey, Ollie. How have you been?"

"All good, auntie. All good."

"Did I wake you up? You sound a little groggy."

"No . . . I mean, yes. You woke me up. I got home from work, and I'm exhausted, so I decided to take a nap." It wasn't exactly a lie, just the job part. If giving a little weed to the neighborhood kids could be considered work, then he was telling the truth. And if smoking a joint could be considered the equivalent of a nap. He supposed they were close enough.

"Oh, I'm so sorry, honey. It's just . . . Vinny won't be able to take care of your cousin Freddy today, and I was wondering if you were free."

Oliver shot up from his bed. "B-But I'm supposed to babysit him next week."

"I know, sweetie, believe me, I wouldn't be asking you this if I had a choice. I work double shifts today, and I don't have anyone else who can take care of Freddy."

Oliver ran his hand over his head, scratching his blond buzz cut. "Okay, auntie, it's fine. I'll stay home, and we can both chill."

"Thank you so much, Ollie. God rewards good deeds."

"Yeah, yeah."

"I'll call you when I drop him off in the house, okay?"

"Alright," Oliver hung up and threw himself on the bed again.

Why did he always have to do everything? His family always had him doing errands and boring shit, not to mention that they would often criticize his habits and his ways of earning money, yet they seldom complained whenever they needed a little extra cash.

Oliver stared at the ceiling of his bedroom, wishing with all his being to be able to disappear. Get rid of all his responsibilities and just chill on a remote island.

His cell phone beeped. It wasn't a call but a text message. He reached out, crawling on the mattress as if his body was made of stone. The screen lit up immediately. Oliver touched the notification icon and a message popped into view. It was from a private number. It showed no names, not even the number itself, only two letters at the bottom of the message, where the sender's name should have been: NV.

The message read:

Hello Sloth.

I've been watching you closely for a while now. You immerse yourself in your own misery, letting the days drag you, throwing away your life for a quick buck, and getting high. Now, let's see how much you actually care for your life and those in it. This is your family, are they not?

A picture showed a group of people gathered at a table. The image seemed to have been taken from outside the house, looking into the window. It was nighttime, and all the members of his family were at the table—his aunt Ana, his cousin Freddy, his other cousin Vinny, his grandfather, and him. The photo must have been taken recently, last Saturday, as Saturdays were the only days when the whole family would sit together to eat. Oliver's heart started beating at a frantic speed, so much that he thought it would come out of his chest at any moment.

Who was this psycho? And why was he stalking Oliver? A wave of scenarios flooded his mind. He thought of calling the police, but maybe it was someone from another gang. It wasn't the most convenient thing in the world to involve the police. Also, if whoever was threatening him knew so much about him and could get close to his family with such ease, who knows what else they would be capable of. He had no other choice but to comply. A second message arrived in the notification app.

If you don't want to see them chopped up into little pieces, I recommend that you do everything I ask.

Oliver's trembling fingers managed to form a question: *What do you want?*

He sent the reply and, a second later, received another message.

I'll send you instructions for your first assignment shortly.

I have to take care of my cousin tonight, Oliver wrote.

Don't worry, the stranger replied. *I'll keep an eye on him.*

LUST

Jessica raised her head back in ecstasy. She saw her own reflection on the ceiling, which was completely covered by a mirror. The dim lights of the hotel room gave a faint orange tint to the place, highlighting the details of their bodies. She was on top of her most recent client, a handsome, rich man whose wife had become rigid over the years. She looked down and dug her nails in the man's well-defined pecs as she rode him. It drove him crazy. The tone of her moans raised, her crotch tightening. The man started to moan too, and she knew he was almost there.

Indeed, a few more thrusts did the trick. The man's eyes went to the back of his head, letting out animalistic grunts as his muscles contracted and then relaxed completely. She stayed there for a few more seconds while the man was panting. He seemed exhausted even though she was the one who did most of the work. She leaned forward and kissed the man on the forehead. His name was Timothy Wilson, a recognizable name in almost the entire state, but that night, with her, he was nothing more than her little pet. She had him at her mercy.

Jessica got off and strode to the bathroom, aware of the gaze fixed on her butt as she walked. She turned on the light, leaving the door ajar. She inspected herself in the mirror, looking for something to fix, but everything seemed to be in place. That new makeup was wonderful. After a session like that, her hair was just a little messy and nothing more. If it weren't because her body was shining in sweat, she might as well have been watching television.

"Wow," Tim gasped from the bed. "The perfect way to end the day."

"I saw you on the news," Jessica said as she approached the bed and dove onto the soft mattress. They still had another hour left, and Tim could be in the mood for a third round. "You looked so confident, giving that speech."

Tim shrugged. "It's because I memorized it. To be honest, I was kind of nervous."

"No, you weren't," she teased. "You should be used to being the center of attention."

A smug smile drew on his face. "I am. It's just that . . . this was one of those few times that I really spoke from the heart, you know?"

"Why is it that men get sentimental after sex?"

Tim shrugged. "I don't know. I haven't had sex with a man, so I can't tell you."

She chuckled. He was a good guy if you glossed over the fact that he was unfaithful to his wife. The truth was that, in her line of work, she didn't usually interact with guys like him. Well, there were many millionaires with super-inflated egos, but most didn't like to talk. Tim did enjoy the talk, and it wasn't just to brag.

"What you did today is very sweet. A charity for children with disabilities. Such a gesture must guarantee you the way to Heaven."

He shook his head. "I didn't do it out of the goodness of my heart. It gave the company a good image, and our stock market shares will definitely rise in value."

"Drop the tough-guy act. I can see right through you like Victoria's Secret lingerie. I know you're a teddy bear deep inside."

He laughed. "Shut up."

"I know how you feel—giving something to someone who needs it. To see the expression of happiness painted across their face and know that you did that. There's no feeling in the world like it."

"Oh, I imagine you've seen many faces of satisfaction."

"Don't be a jerk," Jessica rolled on the bed, facing up. "I mean, you're not the only one who helps the needy."

"What do you mean?"

"Have I ever told you why I'm in this line of work?"

Tim sat on the bed, covering the lower part of his body with the sheet. That was another curious thing about men. Most didn't like to expose themselves when they were flaccid. But the second they got hard, they'd start swinging it around like a sword.

"No, not really," he said. His eyes wandered around the room as if looking for an answer. "I always assumed that it was out of necessity."

"No, honey. I mean, some women do this out of necessity. That's how it started for me. But after I was able to pay for my studies and graduate with honors in business, I started doing it for pleasure."

"You have a business degree?" Tim asked. Rather than surprised, he seemed impressed.

"Yep, Financial Analyst. Now, most of what I earn, I invest. I estimate that I will be able to retire and live off dividends in just a couple of years."

"Smart girl."

"My mom didn't raise a dummy. I started this job because of an ex-boyfriend." Just thinking about him made her stomach turn. She shook the thought of him out of her mind and continued: "I began to make good money and built a reputation. Then it came to a point where I no longer depended on him to get clients. I could choose my own clients. That is more the exception than the rule, but when you've been in this business for as long as I have, you can break a couple of rules. From there, I began to enjoy it. I earned enough to pay the rent, give myself some luxuries, and I had a little left over to invest. And now that I could choose, well, let's say that I no longer saw it as 'selling my body' but as being paid for having sex. You could argue and say it's the same, but the difference is huge for me."

"I find your story interesting so far."

"I know most of your life already, so it's fair that you know a little bit about mine."

"You and anyone who goes on Wikipedia."

"Anyway, one day, one of my regulars arrives. He brought a kid with him."

"A kid?"

"I say kid, but he was already eighteen years old. He had just turned eighteen, actually. But the point is that the boy came in a wheelchair. My client told me that, now that the boy was old enough, he should be able to enjoy a woman. Normally, I don't do that kind of stuff, but I thought it was sort of sweet, so I said fuck it.

The boy could barely move and obviously couldn't walk, but what needed to work worked. So, we went on ahead."

"Lucky kid."

"Very lucky. I made sure to give him the night of his life. We went on for longer than what they'd paid, but I didn't care. To see the expression of that boy's face while we were doing it and the smile from ear to ear he had after we finished. It was one of the most rewarding experiences of my whole life. Being able to feel that I made him happy, even if it was only for one night. I guess that's what you must have felt today."

"Well, I wouldn't compare it to that," he said with a smile. "But you're right. There's no feeling like it."

Jessica's phone vibrated on the nightstand. She was willing to ignore it, but a second beep made her reconsider. Her clients could become a bit clingy at times, but it wasn't wise to let slide something that could be urgent.

"Will you excuse me for a moment?" she asked.

"Sure. Believe me, I know what it's like to have a busy schedule."

Jessica jumped out of bed, grabbed her phone, and went straight to the bathroom. This time, she locked the door. She didn't like to mix her client's time, but since Tim didn't mind, she had the green light.

The message came from an unknown number. In other circumstances, she would have ignored the messages and deleted them without even taking a second look. However, the header of the message caught her eye.

Hi there, Lust.

The sender was also unusual: NV.

Jessica's finger hovered over the screen, hesitant. Her gaze was fixed on the screen while morbid curiosity took hold of her. She tried to fight the impulse, but she lost. Jessica tapped on the icon, and the message manifested on the screen.

Hi there, Lust.

I've wanted to talk to you for a long time. But I had to wait until now. You know your sins. You've succumbed to the desires of your body throughout your entire life. You've never discriminated either. Tall ones, short ones, men, women, black, white. It's all the same to you as long as they give you either money or an orgasm. Tonight, you'll have to face the consequences of your actions. Remember this fellow?

The second message had a photo attached. Jessica swallowed dryly. What kind of sick joke was this? The image that popped up made her blood turn ice cold.

It was Stephen Ross. Her former high school boyfriend, the one who had introduced her to prostitution. The one who tried to convince her to traffic drugs with her friends. The one who hit her, abused her and threatened to kill her almost every night. He had aged. Now he was carrying a beard and dark circles that made him look like a zombie. The photo was candid, and it looked recent. He was walking in the middle of the day on an avenue not far from her favorite hotel. The message that followed read:

It turns out he's in the city. A business trip. Or so he says. It would be a shame if someone were to give him the address of the girl who wronged him so long ago. The one who left him in debt with the other dealers and ran away with another of his girls. Just a guess, but is your address still 72 Cross Street?

Jessica felt the floor crumble beneath her feet. This could not be happening. Not now that everything in her life was in order, not now that she had found some semblance of happiness. She couldn't even begin to imagine what would happen if Stephen found out he was in the same city as her, not only that, if he knew her address. And how was it that this damn creep knew where she lived? Nothing made any sense, but she had to do something. She couldn't let her life be ruined or . . . worse. She was very aware of what Stephen was capable of doing to people who had pissed him off. She didn't even want to begin to imagine what he would do after a decade-old grudge.

Don't do it, she texted. *I will call the police.*

Another message came before she could dial 911.

I know exactly what hotel you are in and which room. Let's see who gets to you first, Stephen or the police. The cops are having a busy night, and Stephen is not far off from you, so I'm willing to put my money on Steve.

Jessica clutched her phone, tempted to throw it against the wall and watch it burst into a thousand pieces, but that would be a very stupid decision and perhaps the last one of her life.

"Hey, Jess!" Tim called. "Is everything alright?"

"Dandy!"

Jessica's hands were sweating so much that her phone started to slide off her fingers. She had no choice. With her heart racing and her face boiling, she typed:

What do you want me to do?

GREED

Roger gripped the bouquet of flowers in his hand. It didn't matter how many times he stepped into the sterile room, flooded with the smell of chemicals and air conditioning, he would never get used to that view.

His mother slept peacefully in the hospital bed. Her silver hair laid on the sheets, slight traces of the blonde she once had on a few strands. She was eighty-three years old, but until about six months ago, she walked, talked, did chores, and many more things than someone her age —hell, someone *his* age— wouldn't be able to do in a single day. But since she had been diagnosed, she had stayed glued to that bed.

She was asleep most of the time, but even when awake, she wasn't always totally lucid. Sometimes, she wouldn't even recognize him. It was the meds; it had to be. Roger refused to believe that his mother was giving away her last few breaths.

He approached the nightstand next to her and switched the already withered flowers for the new ones. She had always loved lilies, and Roger's heart filled with joy every time she woke up to see the flowers beside her and contemplated them in awe as if it were the first time.

Roger sat next to her. Despite the wrinkles, the paleness of her skin, and her gray hair, she was still the beautiful woman who had raised him. The one who scolded him when she found him sniffing around the fridge in the middle of the night, looking for snacks. The one who had taken him to the park every weekend to get some ice cream. The one who'd let him sleep in her room when he couldn't fall asleep.

A warm, almost hot, tear escaped from his eye and slid down his cheek. Roger felt like he was eight years old again, small and helpless, only this time, he had no shoulder to cry on.

Roger had divorced twice, and he had no need to attempt a third time to realize that it was all a big charade. He had left his youth days behind, and finding a compatible partner became more difficult over the years.

After stepping in his forties, it had become almost impossible to date. But he didn't care. Not having children or a wife wasn't something that mattered to him that much. However, the prospect that the only woman who had truly loved him and had always been there for him was going to leave him was unbearable.

The attending physician had proposed an experimental treatment that had shown very promising results. However, the cost of such treatment was just over half a million dollars. Considering her age and the fatality rate of her disease, the insurance company refused to pay for the expenses. He had no choice but to spend all of his savings and what he was currently earning just to keep her alive.

Roger leaned over his chair, reached into his briefcase, and took out his tablet to distract himself. There was a television hanging on the wall, but he didn't want the noise to wake his mother or give her nightmares. He connected the headphones to the device and began searching for some interesting videos to watch. However, just when he was about to tap on the browser. The sound of a notification blasted his ears.

"Jesus, Mary and Joseph," he mumbled. "Why is this thing so loud?"

He saw the icon of his email with a glowing number one on top. His first email in a very long time. Surely spam. Roger tapped on the icon just in case it was a bill he'd forgotten to pay. The dashboard popped up. It was from someone named NV. Roger opened the email.

Howdy, Greed.

A little bird told me about your dilemma. I have a proposal for you. Do as I say, and you'll be rewarded with one million dollars by the end of the week. If you refuse the offer, well, you can slowly watch life extinguish out of your mommy's eyes every single day. I wait for your response—the clock's ticking.

Roger's head jerked back in surprise. He sat silently in shock. What was this guy on about? A million dollars? It sounded like one of those Nigerian prince scams. He wanted nothing to do with that sort of stuff. But still, whoever sent him that message knew about his mother.

He could've guessed, he thought. *Besides, anyone who would take the time to look into my life would eventually find out about my mom. It's not like I have much going on for me at the moment.*

Another notification appeared on his feed. This one was from his bank. Roger's eyes widened. It showed that an anonymous source sent him a check for ten thousand dollars. Roger shot up from his chair, almost dropping the tablet.

There was a second message from NV. This one read:

This is a little gift, just so you know that I'm not full of shit. Ticktock, Greed. I'm waiting for an answer.

Roger ran his hand over his head, jaw hitting the floor. That couldn't be a real notification. It had to be some kind of scam. Roger closed the email application and took out his phone. He could have opened the application from his tablet, but his security had already been compromised, and the last thing in his mind was entering his bank account from the tablet.

Besides, Roger could easily access the account from his cell phone, and he didn't have to connect to a public Wi-Fi network to do so. He wasn't thinking straight at this point. His mind had stopped working, grasping for the hope that it was real. He entered his username and password.

Indeed, a ten thousand dollar transaction was pending. It would become effective the next day. Roger fell back on his seat, his legs rubbery. He decided not to waste a single second and wrote a reply to the text. After receiving that sum of money for just a proposal, it was worth listening to what the guy had to say.

I'm interested.

SLOTH

Oliver's pulse quickened.

He put his hands in the pockets of his jacket while surveying the area. After his aunt had arrived with his cousin Freddy, Oliver had received another message stating that he wouldn't have to worry about little Freddy. His assignment shouldn't take more than an hour. Oliver followed the instructions of the hacker to the letter.

The text led Oliver to a deserted stadium's parking lot. It was a weeknight, with no events scheduled and a hazy climate that wasn't very inviting for outdoor activities. Yet, there they were, just as NV had said.

It was a local gang. Almost all its members wore the corresponding colors, red and white, of the Third Street Soles, a local gang composed mostly of Latinos. Despite their differences, Third Street had reached a truce with Oliver's crew. Although he usually didn't get involved in territory and diplomacy issues, he still had to stick his neck out from time to time to get a good deal.

Those guys knew him. It wasn't like they were best buds, but at least they wouldn't leave him like Swiss cheese for cruising around in their hood. And, to his dismay, what NV had asked him to do was much worse than anything Oliver could've ever imagined.

They were a large group consisting of three cars parked to the side and about twelve of the Third Street members, talking and drinking, with music blaring from the trunk of one of their cars. Oliver kept an eye on a red Cruiser as he swallowed dryly.

NV had ordered him to steal the car.

He had been clenching his pockets tightly, almost tearing the fabric, to stop his hands from shaking. His head jerked from side to side, his own body refusing to do the equivalent of suicide.

I can't do this. I can't.

Oliver turned around and walked away. There was no way. It'd be suicide. On the other hand, if he did nothing, he would be condemning his whole family, and who knew what that lunatic was capable of. There was no turning back.

Oliver stopped. He had to create a distraction.

The group couldn't see him from that angle. Oliver threw himself to the ground and began to roll over it, making sure to cover his clothes in as much dirt and grime as possible. He stood up, put both hands on the side of the building in front of him, and smacked the left side of his face against the brick wall.

The pain made him recoil, but in less than a second, he whipped his head against the wall again and again until the pain became unbearable. His vision blurred. The ground beneath him seemed to move like the tide of the sea. He could feel a warm liquid sliding from his eyebrow to his cheek. It was blood. He was ready.

Oliver staggered toward the gigantic parking lot, flailing his arms like a madman stranded on a deserted island, shouting for help. The group focused their attention on him; eyes widened, some began to curse out loud. One of the gang members, tall in tanned skin, approached him. Oliver recognized him; his name was Ricardo.

"Rico," Oliver gasped. He tried to explain the situation in the best Spanish he could. " Los Santos are in your turf. I saw them, and they ganged up on me. I got away, but who knows what they're up to."

"Up to no good," Rico said. "What were you doing here, anyway?"

"I-I was meeting somebody, okay? It would've been good news for you if I got the deal, but somebody must've snitched to the Santos gang."

"Where'd they go?" asked one of the members behind Rico while the rest jogged closer to them.

"That way!" Oliver pointed to the street behind him. "They took the way under the bridge."

"They won't get far," Rico said. "Those cabrones won't know what hit them."

Without further ado, the group ran in the direction Oliver had pointed. He was kneeling on one leg, pretending to be injured. While the left side of his face hurt like hell, the limp had been improvised.

And the Oscar goes to . . .

As soon as he lost sight of the group, Oliver dashed to the row of cars parked only a few feet away. He looked into one of the cars, searching for any keys they could've left inside. He opened the door and sat in the driver's seat. A light blinked on the dashboard. A set of keys lay on top of it with a miniature teddy bear hanging from them.

He had mistaken them for some sort of toy or adornment at first glance.

Without time to get excited about his accomplishment, Oliver snatched the keys and started the car. The engine roared to life. Oliver closed the door and prepared to get the hell out of there when a scream behind him made him jolt.

"Hey! Somebody's stealing our rides!"

Oliver stepped on the gas. The wheels shrieked on the pavement as the vehicle picked up speed. He swerved around a streetlamp and toward the exit of the parking lot as gunshots blasted in the night. The first few were sporadic, but soon enough, others joined in a deafening cacophony. Sparks flew on the sides of the car. The side mirror exploded with a bang, and the back window broke into a thousand pieces as bullets made their way in from all directions.

Oliver ducked his head as low as he could while still trying to keep his eyes on the road. The car racketed its way to the exit of the parking lot. The bumper of the car broke open the gate and skidded to the avenue as the rain of bullets continued. Oliver was now having a hard time gripping the wheel with his sweaty hands.

He picked up on a ramp leading to the highway. Oliver sighed in relief and rested his head back. His whole body was soaked in his sweat. He got on the fastest aisle and changed speeds, hoping to get as far away as possible from those guys.

His relief was short-lived.

A flare coming from the rear-view mirror blinded him. A large red Sedan was picking up speed behind him. Judging by the speed, it was only a matter of time before they caught up to him, and apparently, they had no intention of having a civil conversation. The car grew in size on the mirror until its bumper was just a few inches from Oliver's trunk. Oliver accelerated.

A blow from behind jerked his head forward, almost knocking him to the wheel. Oliver could feel the adrenaline pumping through his entire body. He thought about bailing out and jumping out of the car, but at that speed and with vehicles behind them, he would only last a couple of seconds before getting mangled on the pavement.

Another hit pushed him forward. They wanted to derail him. He wasn't going to let that happen.

Until then, Oliver had focused almost all of his attention on the car behind him, so he hadn't realized that he was dangerously approaching a Honda in front of him. Just when he realized it, he turned the steering wheel to the other lane, dodging the car by an inch. For a second, he hoped that whoever was following him would not have such quick reflexes to react, but they did, managing to stay behind Oliver as if the cars were tied together. It was then that Oliver had an idea, but it was a bold maneuver. After all, he was no Vin Diesel.

Oliver accelerated until, once again, he was mere inches from another car in front of him, a Toyota. He took a quick glance at the only side mirror he had left, the one on the passenger side, to check if there were any upcoming cars in the other lane. There weren't.

He took a deep breath, wondering if it would be his last. His right hand rested on the emergency brake.

"Alright, bitch! C'mon, let's do this!" He yelled as he pulled the emergency brake and turned to the empty lane.

The car skidded to the side as the wheels shrieked loudly. He turned the steering wheel, making a full circle, and then back to its original position. The car made an effective U-turn in the middle of the highway as the car behind him moved on.

As he had imagined, whoever was chasing him kept going at full speed, crashing headfirst into the Toyota. Both cars seemed like they were ice skating, dancing for a few split seconds. The Toyota derailed, spinning out of control until it stopped completely. The red Sedan followed long; its right side lifted as if it was a balloon. The car rolled over in the air and crashed to the side, turning upside down.

Oliver turned to the right direction of the highway with his heart pumping at full speed and drove past them.

The wheels of the Sedan were now looking up to the night sky, a black wisp of smoke engulfing it and going upward. The Toyota stood in the same spot, its rear demolished. The driver, however, stood outside the car, rubbing his neck and trying to make sense of what had happened. There seemed to be nobody else with him.

Oliver took off before the Toyota guy, or the one in the overturned Sedan, could do anything else. He didn't even check if the one who was chasing him had survived. He'd find out tomorrow on the news if he didn't get caught before that, of course.

With one last sigh of relief, Oliver headed to the address NV had provided to deliver the car.

Vin Diesel ain't got shit on me.

PRIDE

Timothy helped his wife set the table for dinner, as they did religiously every night. He put four cloth napkins, one in front of each chair, with the utensils carefully positioned to the side. Linda, on the other hand, was finishing the meal before putting it on the table. It wasn't a banquet. After all, Linda had an accurate idea of how much each food the rest of the family could take. Cooking was a gift God had given her, and Tim couldn't deny that. It is often said that a way to a man's heart is through his stomach, but, despite his wife's extraordinary culinary skills, that had never been the case with Tim. Although, if he was honest with himself, he had trouble remembering what made him attracted to her in the first place. She was beautiful, of course, but there had to be something more.

Once their work was finished, Timothy called out for his children to come down. The girl, Wendy, sat down first with the elegance of a queen. She was the oldest, but even though she was only two years older than her brother, Jamie, it felt like there was a ten-year gap between them. Jamie pushed the chair away and sat down without even looking up, his eyes glued to the device he carried in his hands. The familiar sounds of his video game echoed in the dining room.

"Put that away, Jamie," said Tim. "We're going to eat."

Jamie glanced up for a split second. "Just a sec, Dad, I'm about to beat my score."

Always ambitious.

"You have until your mom serves the food."

First was Wendy's plate. The girl beamed a smile when she saw the mashed potatoes, her favorite. Jamie was the second to receive his plate. Then, Tim and Linda sat down with her own dish being the last. Linda reached her hands to her husband and daughter and held them, ready to give thanks.

Tim leaned over the table and snapped his fingers in front of Jamie. "Hey buddy, time's up."

"I just need one second," the boy begged.

Linda sighed in frustration. Tim wouldn't hear the end of it if he didn't put his foot down. He snatched the smartphone out of his son's hand and put it in his pocket.

"Hey!" Jamie yelled.

"I warned you," said Tim.

He grabbed his wife and son's hands. The four closed their eyes while Linda thanked God for putting bread on their table. Once the prayers were over, they began to eat. Tim was the first to break the silence; he loved to hear Wendy's stories about school. She always had something to say.

"How was school today, honey?"

Wendy finished chewing and swallowed with the help of some orange juice before answering. "It was good. Mr. Prickly said he saw . . ." The girl paused to remember the exact words the teacher had used and then said, "artistic potential in me."

Linda and Tim exchanged looks of amazement and pride.

"Really?" Linda asked. "Was it because of the drawing you made as a project?"

"Yep," she said with emotion. "He liked it so much that he'll put it on the classroom's billboard for the rest of the year."

Tim had seen it. He had been the one who took Wendy to buy the crayons. The girl had drawn a bouquet of flowers full of lilies, roses, violets, and a sunflower. The truth was that it looked very impressive for someone her age, hell, even for someone his age. There was nothing Wendy wouldn't excel at.

"Congratulations, honey," Tim said without making any effort to hide his pride. "You deserve your mashed potatoes and a visit to the park this weekend."

The girl's cheeks blushed as her smile widened. "Thank you, daddy."

Tim turned to Jamie. "What about you, champ?"

Jamie's eyes widened. "Nothing new."

"He was sent to detention," Wendy said.

"Shut up!" Jamie shouted.

Linda glared at Jamie, her eyes on fire. "Is that true?"

Jamie did not answer.

"James Wilson, answer your mother when she speaks to you," Tim ordered.

The boy's face flushed; he was so focused on his plate that it looked like he was going to dig his face into the food.

"Why do you have to ruin everything?" the boy snapped at his sister, grabbed a handful of mashed potatoes, and threw it at Wendy.

The girl shouted as the food hit her on the chest, brown gravy spraying all over her.

Tim shot up. Jamie jumped off his chair and ran to his room.

"Come back here!" Tim shouted. A second later, he heard the door slamming shut upstairs.

Tim took a deep breath and let out a sonorous sigh. Linda was cleaning Wendy's dress, who had now started to bawl her eyes out.

"It's okay, honey," Linda said in a smooth voice, almost a whisper. "He didn't really mean it."

"Look at what he did to my dress!" The girl complained and started sobbing again.

"We'll clean it," Tim said as he stepped off the table. "If not, I'll buy you a new one."

That didn't seem to calm her, but he didn't care. She'd be okay and smiling after a few minutes and a shower. Jamie, on the other hand, was a different issue. Tim climbed the stairs to the second floor of the penthouse and pondered for a minute in front of his son's door. He raised his fist, ready to knock on the wooden door when a noise startled him. A hissing sound came from his private study.

Tim felt compelled to investigate, his legs moving on their own to the study room. The only light in the room was the bluish hue of his computer monitor, which he remembered to have turned off a few hours ago. The noise, however, came from the fax machine right next to it. Once it was done printing, the lone page glided in the air and landed gracefully at his feet. It displayed a single message: *Check your email.*

As if it had a life of its own, the Internet browser opened by itself on the screen. The homepage appeared, inviting Tim to the unknown. He swallowed and gave hesitant steps toward his chair.

He sat down and opened the email, trying not to think about the ramifications of what was happening, yet he couldn't help it. If someone was hacking into his computer, they probably had his email's password because the browser had already memorized the username and password. With remote control over the device, the guy didn't even need Tim to access the mail but still seemed to want Tim to do it by himself. He was probably trying to give Tim a false sense of security or control.

But it's not gonna happen, asshole. As soon as I know what this is about, I'm going to call the police.

He glanced at the last email in the inbox. It had a picture attached. He clicked on it, and his jaw dropped at the sight.

There were about five photos of him, taken from outside a hotel window. One of him taking off his clothes, another with Jess, the escort he frequented. The other three images were more explicit. They showed Tim and Jess engaging in different sexual positions.

Timothy felt his blood boil. Who could have the audacity to stalk him like that? Getting their noses into his personal life? Does this guy not know who Timothy Wilson is? What he's capable of? Timothy snatched his phone, ready to dial 911, when an idea struck him. If whoever was behind this was capable of hacking into his personal computer, then who knows what other information they could have gotten. Tim put the phone down and read the email.

Greetings, Pride.

I know what you're thinking. And before you decide to do something drastic, I recommend you to consider this: I'm not going to get caught. I made sure to cover my tracks effectively. And even if, for some twist of fate, I were to get caught, it wouldn't make a difference for me. I already live in my own personal prison. I have nothing left to lose. You, however, have a lot to lose: your company, your family, your prestige. Imagine what would happen if the wrong person were to see those pictures, like your wife, for example. I hope the contract you signed when you married covered a situation like this so she won't strip you of everything you own. But I doubt that. After all, you married young and in love. If these pictures go public, there won't be anything left of you but an empty shell.

You need to not worry, though. I'll make sure to delete them and any information I have about you, which includes a few instances of fraud and tax evasion depending on who you ask, if and only if you do precisely as I say.

Do I have your cooperation?

Timothy froze, unable to fully process what he had just read. It was true, everything he had said. If his wife were to find out about his escapades, it would be game over for him. With the right lawyer, she could take everything. And knowing that bitch, it would be exactly what she'd do, but not before taking the children too. The media would tear him apart. Everything he had built over ten arduous years would fall apart in a matter of a couple of months. He couldn't let that happen. He had to trust the word of this man and expect him to fulfill his part of the deal. Most likely, he was extorting Tim for money. And Tim would comply; he'd give all the money the hacker asked for in order to have peace of mind.

Tim tapped his response on the keyboard:

Miguel Estrada

Deal.

GREED

Roger received the instructions from the hacker soon after accepting the offer. It sounded too good to be true, like those scams plastered all over the Internet. However, in none of the horror stories he had heard about hackers or scammers had he heard of someone who sent the "victim" ten thousand dollars in advance. This didn't sound like any scam; it was definitely a job offer, and it made sense that whoever wanted the job done would use illicit methods to request it. Even so, his assignment sounded a bit too easy for the amount of money he had been offered. He was sure that even an amateur would be able to carry it out.

Roger climbed the steep hill leading to the lonely house at the end of the street. Every step he took seemed to take him further and further away from civilization., and the houses became increasingly separated from each other. The light from the streetlamps dwindled until he was almost covered in the shadows. He had reached a point where the moonlight was his guide, a silvery orb shining brightly in the clear sky.

He stopped at the mailbox of the property where he had been assigned to go, 137 Warren Ave. The hill grew steeper toward a clearing surrounded by trees and a dirt road that meandered to a huge house. It was so big that it might as well have been a mansion with boarded windows, moldy walls, and a state of decay that implied that no one had set foot there in ages.

Roger pulled out the piece of paper where he had written the address to double-check that he was in the right place. He wondered why someone would send him to rob a house in such a bad condition. It didn't even seem to be inhabited.

Roger assumed it looked that way because of its owner. According to what NV had informed him, the owner was an old veteran who had lost his sight due to glaucoma. Roger had been tasked to go to the attic and steal all the contents of a chest. When Roger asked what he should be looking for, NV replied that Roger could simply take everything inside or the whole chest if necessary.

Roger prayed not to meet any hell hounds this time as his boots dug deep in the dirt with every step.

As soon as he reached the porch of the house, a chill ran down his spine. The place was even more disturbing up close. No window seemed accessible, every inch covered by wooden boards. A barred door stood just in front of the wooden door with a metal padlock. Whoever this guy was, he liked his privacy. Roger walked around the house, scanning the structure in search of an access point.

A noise coming from what should be the kitchen stopped him. Instinctively, he ducked but then remembered the owner of the house was blind, so it wouldn't make much of a difference to hide. However, that created a different dilemma.

He had read somewhere that when you are deprived of any of your senses, the others became sharper to compensate. There were blind people who could place a mosquito in a room just because of the sound it made or perceive changes in the air around it. Scary shit, no doubt.

Okay, no biggie. I just have to be more quiet than usual.

Roger's eyes met a basement door at the foot of the house. Bingo. It didn't seem to be as protected as the main entrance, and the truth was that accessing through there was easier than most people thought. He approached and saw that it was sealed by a simple lock. Piece of cake. He just had to make sure not to make much noise.

He bent over one knee, took out the lock pick, and worked his magic.

In a matter of minutes, it was open. He heard a faint, almost inaudible metallic click, put the lock on the floor, and opened the right side of the door.

The rusted hinges chirped. Roger stopped and proceeded to open it more carefully, his pulse almost surgical. Once finished, he entered the darkness of the basement.

Beams of moonlight crept through the cracks on the top of the walls. The sound of dripping water, accompanied by the smell of decay and moisture, made him want to abandon his mission. He wasn't squeamish, but there was something about that house that triggered all of his red flags. He took out his flashlight and turned it on. The beam of light could barely illuminate a fraction of his surroundings. Roger did a quick scan to get familiar with the environment. He found the usual: boxes, crates, and a rusty bike.

What did I expect? Find a dead body?

The possibility that it could be a trap had not even crossed his mind. It could all be part of an elaborate maneuver to leave him isolated in the dark with some dude wanting to bash his skull in.

Except that didn't make any sense; whoever was behind the creepy messages had already paid him a good sum of money just to break into the place. Someone that loaded could use the spare cash to send a hitman if they wanted to see him dead. No, this went beyond anything he could imagine.

Without even really looking, Roger found the stairs leading up. Each step he took was silent, trying to place his foot in the wood like a feather.

But then, he reached the last step.

The weathered wood creaked, spreading a spectral echo. Roger froze in the dark without realizing that he had stopped breathing. He became attentive to any sound, any indication that the owner of the house had noticed his presence. But nothing happened. Roger stood in place for around five minutes before deciding to take the last step to the first floor.

Roger made his way through the dark veil of the night, guided by his flashlight and his hand sliding down the wall. He reached the living room. A solitary piece of furniture with a table in front and an old radio were the only things in the ample space. To his right, stairs led to the second floor, and to his left, a doorless frame to the kitchen. Roger crept toward the stairs, his ears ringing due to the abrasive silence. It was then he heard a click behind him.

Roger's blood froze instantly. He managed to contain a scream, and his heart started racing. Slowly, he turned over his shoulder. What he saw made him want to run away as far as possible.

A dark figure stood at the entrance of the kitchen, carrying what appeared to be a shotgun with both hands. The figure stepped forward. The gun shone under the light of his flashlight. The figure was a bald man with a gray beard, his crystalline eyes staring at nothing.

The veteran cocked his head to the side as if sharpening his hearing. Roger noticed that the old man's nostrils opened and closed erratically.

Does he smell me?

Roger stayed in place without moving a muscle and swallowed.

The man turned his head in the direction Roger was and began to walk toward him. Roger thought about throwing the flashlight into the hallway leading to the basement, but then he'd be completely blind in uncharted territory. Not to mention that the madman with the shotgun should have a mental map of his own house, so outsmarting him that way wasn't going to happen. Roger tucked his hand in his pocket and pulled the jackknife lockpick out.

Goodbye, my old friend, he thought as he threw the jackknife in the opposite direction.

The tool clanged on the other side of the living room. In that deafening silence, it sounded like he had dropped a bomb. The man lunged toward the source of the sound. Roger bent on his knees and untied his shoes. He took them off and left them at the bottom of the stairs. Now barefoot, he climbed the stairs skipping three steps at a time.

Roger reached the second floor and raised the flashlight toward the ceiling, desperately searching for some mechanism to reach the attic. Thankfully, the light uncovered what he was looking for. In the middle of the hall was the attic's retractable ladder. Roger went for it at a brisk pace, stealing glances over his shoulder every couple of seconds.

He pulled the ladder down, climbed into the attic, grabbed the ladder from the top, and pulled up, effectively locking himself inside. The staircase closed with a thunderous sound, but the blind man should not be able to reach the attic as long as Roger had the cord up with him.

Roger felt tempted to take a second to recover the air, but that could mean death if the veteran found another way up to the attic.

It took Roger half a second to find the chest that NV had mentioned. It was gathering dust right in the middle of a mountain of boxes. He clenched his backpack, praying so that whatever was there was light enough to carry. He knelt and opened the chest. Roger felt a knot in his stomach.

His prayers were not answered.

Inside the chest was a collection of high-caliber weapons: A pump-action shotgun, an AK-47, an M16, two ammunition boxes, and several sidearms that he didn't even bother trying to identify.

Without wasting any more time, Roger took off his backpack and stuffed it with all the sidearms he found. He struggled to fit the ammo boxes inside but managed to do it after shoving them in, stretching the backpack's fabric.

The zipper barely closed. He put it back on his shoulders and felt the straps pulling him down due to the considerable weight. Now the problem was how he was going to load the rifles and the shotgun.

Roger bit his lip as he pondered. He also had to think of a way to get out safely with all of that stuff on him.

Heavy steps echoed around the house, shaking the floor. The blind veteran shouted from the basement.

"Where are you? You son of a bitch! I'll find you and blow your brains out!"

Roger had no doubt that the old man intended to keep his promise. Roger grabbed the shotgun and hung it over his already sore shoulder, put the flashlight in his mouth, and held it with his teeth as he snatched a rifle with each hand. He felt as if he was carrying twice his own body weight. He crawled to the retractable ladder and peered down between the cracks of the door.

He couldn't see much, but he could hear the veteran's footsteps approaching. They were calculated and weighty. Roger held his breath as a figure appeared and stopped in the middle of the hallway. The man bent his knees. Judging by his posture and how firm his grip on the shotgun was, there was no doubt in Roger's mind that the man had been in the military.

Roger felt his pulse quicken when the man lifted the shotgun's barrel up, pointing straight at the attic. The blind man placed his finger on the trigger. Roger pulled the cord and fell down with the ladder. The ceiling collapsed on top of the veteran, the attic door hitting him in the forehead as Roger crashed on his back. The metal ladder slid down and almost pinned Roger to the floor.

Roger stood up like lightning and ran. The blind man was rolling on the floor, rubbing his head in pain. Roger dashed full speed down the stairs to the first floor and then to the basement. He tripped over the last steps and fell to his knees on the muddy ground. He sprang up and staggered his way out, finally able to see the moonlight illuminating the path he came from.

Instead of flaking around the house, Roger ran straight toward the trees, hoping to get lost in the woods and find his way back to civilization once he was far enough from the mad man with the shotgun.

As if summoned, the blind man jumped out of the basement door and fired into the air. The roar of the shotgun shook the night, and Roger ran faster than he had ever thought possible. The man fired a second time blindly.

The trunk of a tree on Roger's left exploded into a thousand pieces. Roger started zigzagging his way around the trees, certain that the next shot would hit him. He waited for the third shot but instead heard the man shouting at the top of his lungs.

"Come back, you coward! Stealing from a blind man! You piece of shit!"

He was right, Roger was a coward, but at least he had survived his ordeal.

LUST

It had not been long since Jessica had received that dreadful text. The hacker, referring to himself as NV, told her that tonight was the night.

Extortion. That's what this was all about. And she couldn't even risk going to the police. She had a history, one that the man blackmailing her from behind a keyboard knew all too well. There was no other option at the moment but to do whatever this NV guy wanted and then disappear. She could open new bank accounts, find a new place to live and change every goddamn password.

NV had instructed her to go to a club downtown called Blue Lagoon. Once there, she would receive further instructions. The hacker had also mentioned that he was looking forward to seeing her in action and using her "gifts."

I swear if all this guy wants is a freebie, I'm going to cut his dick off.

Jessica stood in front of the Blue Lagoon's purple neon lights; despite being a weekday, the entrance was brimming with activity. There was a long line that crossed the corner of the block. She had no time to waste. She went straight to the entrance, striding toward the club's security guard. Cutting in line wasn't something she was used to doing; that was one of the things that her clients usually did. She'd always considered it douchey but understood that if you had enough money, you could basically do whatever you pleased.

She moved her hips gracefully as she made her way through the crowd, feeling all eyes on her. Her heels gave her three more inches, her tight dress accentuating her slender figure. She tried to enter as if she owned the place but was stopped by a giant, sausage-fingered hand right above her chest.

"Where do you think you're going, sugar?" the guard asked, his expression stern and rigid. "If you want to get in, go back in line."

This is going to be harder than I expected.

"I'm Kathy," she lied. There was always a Katherine, or Kate, or Kat. She figured it was her best shot. "I'm one of the performers, and I'm running late, so if you'll excuse me . . ."

She tried to enter again before being gently pushed back by the guard. He didn't even have to put in any effort; he could knock her back with just one finger if he wanted to.

"Look," she started. "I don't have time for this bull . . ."

"She's with me," declared someone behind her.

She turned to see a tall, blue-eyed gentleman with two bodyguards at his sides. He wore an immaculate white suit with a black tie. He seemed young, in his early thirties, but with the attitude of someone who owned the whole world. She was familiar with that kind of man but rarely were they as good-looking as him.

The guard straightened his back. "Mr. Vines. Goodnight, sir."

The man put his hand on Jessica's back and kissed her on the cheek. "Sorry, I'm late. There was traffic."

"It's okay," she managed to say, barely able to play along. She was dumbfounded.

Mr. Vines turned to the guard. "Is there a problem, Felipe?"

The guard locked his eyes on Jessica and, after a second of hesitation, jerked his head. "No, sir. No problem at all."

Mr. Vines smiled. "Good, now if you'd please let us in."

"Of course," Felipe said as he stepped aside and opened the door to them.

They went in. The exposed brick walls reflected the neon lights as they made their way through the hallway.

"Thanks," said Jessica, feeling both grateful but condescended at the same time.

I could've done it by myself.

"It was my pleasure," the man said over the sound of the music. "A beautiful woman like you is welcome in my club, any time."

Jessica's eyes widened. "Your club? You're the owner?"

"Sure am," he replied. He turned to her and winked. "And I *know* you're not one of my girls. But don't worry, as I said, you're more than welcome here. Women like you bring more clientele. Think of it as your own private ladies' night."

Jessica didn't know what to say. She opened her mouth but closed it again.

"Whatever you're going to say, save it. You don't have to keep thanking me or do anything for me either." They reached the main bar. There were two sets of stairs to the side, one going up and another one going down to the dance floor with a DJ on the opposite side of a sea of people having the time of their lives. "Go on, and do whatever you came here to do."

"Huh?"

He leaned in over to her ear. "I know your type. You're not here to have fun. You're on a mission. I can see it in your eyes. Determination. So don't let me stop you. Go get 'em, tiger."

He gave her a pat on the back and left. His two bodyguards followed him like trained dogs. She watched him go up a set of stairs that led to a VIP area. What the hell had happened? She had to admit; not many men impressed her the way he did.

Okay, let's do this.

She went to the ladies' room and locked herself in one of the stalls. She pulled her phone out of her purse and texted.

I'm in.

She waited for the reply, struggling to resist the temptation of biting her freshly painted nails. A message popped up.

Look for this ugly fella. His name's Luis Roca. Try to get close to him and ask him where Los Santos' hideout is. He probably won't talk right away, so use your talents.

Attached to the image was the picture of a chubby, Hispanic-looking guy. He had a tattoo on his face that seemed to come from his neck and had a ring on every finger of both hands. Jessica simply replied with: *Got it.*

She stepped out of the stall and looked at herself in the mirror. Maybe she needed a bit more style. She placed her hand purse on the sink and began to accentuate her makeup. A little more mascara and eyeliner should do the trick. A brighter lipstick wouldn't hurt either. She washed her lips with a wet tissue wipe and painted them in a more extravagant red. When she was done, she put the tools back on the purse, ruffling her own hair a little bit to make it look a bit messy, and raised her dress a little more to her thighs.

Once out of the restroom, her gaze scanned the club. The shining, blinking lights made it hard to distinguish people's faces, let alone their features. She could spend all night trying to find the guy, and it'd be like trying to find a needle in a haystack. To get to him, she had to think like him. At the moment, the only thing she knew about him was how he looked, but if he was like ninety percent of men with power, then he'd probably be wherever there was booze and women.

Jessica squeezed between the people as she explored the club. She went up the stairs to the second floor where she'd seen Vines go earlier. To her surprise, the floor was divided into three sections. All private areas. If she wanted a free ticket in, she'd have to turn some heads. There were a few dance poles with platforms scattered throughout the place, some of them with girls dancing seductively.

She looked around, trying to find Vines, but he didn't seem to be there, which was strange considering how she'd seen him go up there not a minute ago.

He's the owner, dumbhead. He probably has his own private room where he can see everything without moving a finger.

Realizing that she couldn't count on him to further her little operation, she decided to take matters into her own hands. It didn't take her long to figure out that she was right, and the guy she was looking for was sitting on the private lounge with the biggest bar and at least five times more women. Catching his attention was probably going to be difficult, but she enjoyed a challenge.

She left her heels and hand purse at her feet, climbed the nearest platform, and grabbed the pole. The cold metal felt familiar in her hands. She grinned. It had been years since she had to perform like this. Jessica took a deep breath and hoped she was still half as good as she was back then.

Jessica started moving her hips from side to side, getting a feel for the music blasting through the speakers. She closed her eyes and let her body succumb to the rhythm. Her feet moved gracefully. Her hands moved up and down the pole. She stole a glance at where Roca was and caught him checking her out. She smiled and winked as she continued to dance. It was working.

Her dance moves were nothing like the twerking that was all over the place nowadays; it was more subtle, more sensual. And that drove men crazy, the teasing. She knew it all too well. She wrapped her leg around the pole and spun around it, making sure the guy had a full view of the entirety of her body.

Lo and behold, soon enough, Luis Roca was on his feet and briskly walking toward her. She kept dancing as if she hadn't seen him. It was only after he stepped outside the VIP area that she locked eyes with him; she had him.

He stepped closer until he was at her feet.

"You!" Luis Roca demanded. "Come here!"

"Me?" Jessica asked with feigned surprise.

"Yes, you!" he repeated, signaling her to get down from the platform as he eyed her up and down.

Jessica obeyed, put her high heels on, and grabbed her purse. "Where are you taking me?"

He jerked his head to the VIP area. "To where the big guys hang out."

She put her hand on his shoulder. "Why don't we go somewhere more private?"

Luis Roca stayed quiet, his gaze fixed on her with a stone-like expression. For a second, she feared that he'd figure out what she was trying to do. She bit her lip, not as a seductive gesture but trying to conceal her nervousness.

He grinned. "Oh, I see. I see what you want. You're one of the really bad ones, huh?" Roca looked her up and down again. "How much for the night?"

"Well, I can be expensive, but I give a discount to clients I'm truly attracted to." It wasn't a lie. What she failed to mention was that he wasn't one of those clients.

"We'll figure out the price later," he said. He signaled a couple of guys standing around; they nodded and walked toward them. "C'mon, guys! We're leaving."

Jessica couldn't help but smile.

I've still got it.

PRIDE

Timothy drove through the empty road in the dead of night. The headlights only illuminated a few feet in front of the car while the rest of the world remained shrouded in darkness. Even with the windows closed, he could smell the dry air of the desert inside his car. He'd been driving for at least thirty minutes, and it'd been twenty since the last time he'd seen another car.

Where's this guy taking me? Tim wondered.

Tim clenched the steering wheel tightly. What if this was a trap? What if it was some sort of ruse to get him alone in the middle of nowhere and get him killed? Well, he'd rather die than see everything he's worked for his entire life crumble. Besides, who would have taken all of that trouble? Timothy Wilson had a couple of enemies for sure, and probably more than a few people who hated his guts, but there seemed to be something else at play. Extreme measures had been taken, and if anybody wanted to hurt him so badly, they could've simply sent the pictures to everybody he knew and left it at that. Boom. Life ruined at the press of a button.

Tim checked the GPS on his phone and found that he was getting close to where NV had told him to go. The mark seemed to be a bit far off the road, though, and there didn't seem to be any dirt roads for him to follow. It was as if someone had picked a random place in the middle of the desert.

He parked to the side, contemplating if he should continue on foot or with the car. He could keep the engine running, and if there was any sign of a trap, he could always run and take the car back to the road. If he drove to the spot, the way back could be a little more daunting. His car was low, so all it took was a rock hitting on the wrong place to fuck him over and leave him stranded. Being half an hour away from civilization wasn't a comforting thought either.

Tim kept the keys in and opened the trunk. What lay inside the trunk shocked him. He'd simply been told to go to the appointed location and use whatever was in the trunk to find what he was looking for, like some form of a twisted treasure hunt. NV never made it clear what the "treasure" was. But since there was a shovel and a flashlight inside the trunk, Tim figured he was going to dig it out.

Whatever was buried down there had to be something very dangerous or very important. Probably both.

Tim took a deep breath. He grabbed the shovel and the flashlight and closed the trunk. Who would've known that the desert was so freaking cold? He had only walked for a couple of minutes and was already freezing.

Tim's cell phone vibrated in his back pocket. He took a quick glance at it, the screen blinding him for a second. He stood in the exact position that NV had sent him. Now the only thing left to do was to start digging.

Timothy began, swallowing his pride and some sand in the process. Each thrust was more laborious than the previous one. For Timothy, it felt like hours waiting to hear the clinging of metal, leading to some kind of chest, but instead, he heard a thud accompanied by a crack as if he'd hit the root of a tree. Whatever it was that he was supposed to dig out, he probably broke it.

Timothy cussed out his frustration and bent on one knee. Then, a stench unlike anything he'd ever smelled before hit him like a truck. He winced in disgust. That treasure had clearly passed its expiration date.

Tim swallowed dryly and kept digging, more carefully this time.

There was something small, like the size of a baseball bat, wrapped in a black trash bag. Tim covered his face with his forearm as he picked up the strange object. It folded in half as he raised it and put it on the ground.

NV had requested a picture. The foul scent was now unbearable. Tim stuck one of his fingers in the plastic bag and pulled, ripping it a little, enough to see inside. He pointed the flashlight toward the bag. His whole body jolted up, the heel of his feet hitting the edge of the hole. Tim fell to his back, dragging himself away from what he'd seen.

Inside the bag, there was a pale piece of decaying flesh. Its muscles and part of the bone were exposed. He'd only seen a fraction of it, but it didn't take him long to connect the dots.

Timothy was staring at a severed arm.

His fingers dug in the sand. He wanted to get up and run, but his legs had turned rubbery, barely responsive. The cold air of the desert swept over him. What kind of sick fuck would do something like this? Was he going to end up like that? Timothy shook those thoughts out of his mind.

Hyperventilating and sweating buckets, Tim pulled out his phone and snapped a picture. He sent it, hoping to wake up in his bed, next to Linda. Instead, a beeping sound startled him. He had received a message:

Good. Dig out the rest and take it to the address I've sent to the GPS. Get rid of the bags and leave them there. Take pictures. Don't get caught.

What in the actual fuck? Was this guy insane? For the first time in the whole night, a thought crossed his mind, one that surprisingly hadn't come before. He pushed the callback button on NV's number and flattened the phone against his ear. To his surprise, it started ringing.

Someone picked up, but there was only silence at the other end of the line. Timothy exploded.

"What the fuck are you thinking? I can't do this! What if I get caught? Who the fuck are you?"

A robotic, monotone voice answered: "You possess the gift of free will. You can do as you please and leave. But don't be surprised when your face hits the headlines by tomorrow morning. If you do as I say, you'll get to keep the charade you're so fond of. I expect the pictures by midnight. If I don't receive them, then you'll have made yourself clear."

NV hung up. Timothy slammed the phone to the ground and screamed at the top of his lungs. His voice echoed in the silence of the night.

After taking a few deep breaths, filling his lungs with rotten air, Tim stood up and snatched his phone from the sand. He dialed the number one more time. There had to be something else he could do, anything except this madness. A female bot voice replied at the other side of the line:

"The number you're trying to reach is no longer avai—"

"Fuck!" he shouted as he hung up.

He had no choice.

It took him another half an hour and several attempts not to throw up to finally bring all the pieces out. Even then, it was evident that it wasn't the whole corpse. He had taken out one entire arm, part of one leg, and the foot of the other, along with what seemed to be a head. But the torso, the thigh of the right leg, one arm, and the entire left leg seemed to be missing. On the other hand, he was sure there were no more parts missing, so whoever had dismembered the corpse probably hid the rest somewhere else. Timothy wasn't sure if it was a clever strategy or a dumb one.

Tim took the parts one by one to the trunk of the car. Once he was finished, he sat at the driver's seat and slammed the door shut. He let his forehead rest on the steering wheel and started to sob.

How could he have gone so far? Where had his life gone wrong? Was it the cheating? His dull marriage? Maybe he should've never married. Maybe he should have never become a public figure. After all, well-known people always seemed to attract a fair share of wackos like some sort of magnet. He couldn't place the exact moment he had taken the first step toward the path of failure, but there was no reason to ponder on it anyway. He didn't become a millionaire and achieved everything he'd ever dreamed of by feeling sorry for himself. He wiped the tears off his face and turned on the engine.

His fingers went instinctively to the GPS. The location appeared on the screen, leading him to the city, specifically a neighborhood near downtown.

"There has to be a mistake," he told himself.

The device was sending him straight to somebody's house, not only that but to their backyard. Did NV really want him to put dismembered parts of a corpse in somebody's yard in the middle of the city?

There could only be one explanation: Timothy Wilson wasn't the only one playing a pawn in NV's games.

GLUTTONY

Matthew threw his towel on the couch while walking around naked in the living room. The unmistakable smell of soap after a good shower was soothing. He felt the hot water still dripping off his back on his way to the kitchen, his own personal sanctuary. A reflection in the hallway mirror made him pause and admire his naked torso. The muscles of his shoulders accentuated effortlessly, along with the thickness of his biceps that caught the attention of men and women alike. His stomach, however, was not exactly toned. While he didn't have a beer belly, the six-pack he wore with pride in his twenties had completely disappeared, no doubt the results of his eating habits. He shrugged, figuring it was well worth it.

As a cook, he never understood the type of person who liked to cook but not eat. In his mind, a real chef was someone who could not only cook well but be delighted by the variety of flavors the world had to offer.

And today was a special night. He had a date with a young man who had a somewhat . . . peculiar interest. They met online, in one of those Internet forums you'd delete from the browser history after visiting. Matthew took it one step further by having a VPN service, or virtual private network, to hide his IP address, along with using a browser that allowed anonymous navigation. After all, he had to keep his dirty hobby a secret.

Normally, he didn't take his "dates" directly to his house to meet; that would be very risky. But they rarely offered themselves to be the main course. It was as if the chicken went straight to your house, plucked itself, cut its own head, and jumped in the oven.

The guy's name was Oswaldo, a twenty-seven-year-old man with depression and suicidal tendencies who, by the hand of fate, had the particular fetish of being eaten by someone else. Matthew's mouth salivated at the thought, barely able to contain his cravings. He put on his boxers and an apron and began to prepare everything to have it ready when Oswaldo arrived.

Matt put the cell phone aside and turned it off as he didn't like to have any distractions in the kitchen. He took out the pots he was going to use and turned on the oven to preheat it when the phone rang.

Matt grunted, hating to be interrupted.

He strode out of the kitchen to the living room, grabbed the landline phone on the wall, fearing that Oswaldo had gotten cold feet. Matthew had promised him that he wouldn't kill him, that he would first let Oswaldo enjoy his fetish. They both would have a buffet that night before the moment of truth. However, instead of his date's low but shy voice, he found a cold, robotic voice greeting him.

"Hello, Gluttony."

"Gluttony?" Matt recoiled. "Who's this?"

"I'm someone who knows your deepest secrets."

"Oswaldo, if that's you, cut the shit."

"Oswaldo won't be coming over tonight, I'm afraid," said the eerie voice.

"Who the fuck is this?" Mathew repeated.

"I know about your . . . insatiable appetite."

Matthew was about to hang up but supposed it was better to put this guy in his place if he didn't want to be bothered anymore.

"Look, ass-hat, I'm going to hang up, and if you call me ever again, I swear I'm going to–" He was interrupted by the robotic man, who had started to recite a set of random numbers. "Is this some kinda prank? Do you get off on this or what?"

"The number I gave you," said the man on the line. "Those are the coordinates of where you hid your latest victim's corpse, Sarah O'Reilly. The leftovers, at least."

Matthew's face paled. He felt as if someone had just punched him in the gut. "W-What?"

"I'm not going to repeat myself. If you don't want to spend the rest of your life in a jail cell, you'll do exactly as I say."

"Bullshit!" Matthew spat. "You don't know anything. You hear me!"

"Go to your backyard."

Matthew's heart skipped a beat. The only other times in his life where he had felt something so primal was when he killed his victims. The anticipation, the act itself, and the relishing moment of eating their flesh. But now, he was feeling something different yet just as primal: Fear.

He crept to the dining room and stared at his own reflection on the glass, looking to his backyard. The lights outside were off.

Nothing but darkness could be seen beyond a few feet. He raised his hand and flipped on the light switch.

A beam of light illuminated the grim scenario. On his patio, next to the coffee table and beach chairs he'd set up for family gatherings and his Sundays off were parts of what was once a human being, one he recognized as Sarah O'Reilly, whom he still had part of her thigh in his freezer. Her arm lay on one of the chairs, her left foot was down on the ground, and one leg was crossed on top of the coffee table. But it was her head that made his stomach turn; she was looking at him with the same expression of horror and shock as when she drew her last breath. Her face was pale with signs of decay.

The robotic voice broke the silence. "Do I have your attention now?"

Matthew felt a knot in his throat. "Yes."

"I need you to kidnap someone for me. Since you have experience in such matters."

Matthew stood quietly for a moment before asking. "Male or female?"

LUST

Jessica was holding Luis Roca's arm; his two trusted bodyguards at their sides. The four of them strode through the parking lot to a current-year Mercedes Benz. The bodyguards took the driver and passenger seats while Roca and Jessica sat on the back.

It took them a few minutes to reach Roca's hotel, but it felt like hours to Jessica. Roca wouldn't shut up about how influential he was, how he could have anybody do whatever he wanted with a snap of his fingers. Jessica simply nodded and smiled, widening her eyes whenever he said something that was supposed to sound impressive. To her, bragging was nothing more than a poor effort to fish for compliments.

It was a five-star hotel. With marble walls, huge chandeliers, and ninety percent of the structure seemed to be made out of glass. She had to admit; she liked the flashiness of it all. They went straight to the elevator to the top floor, where the suite waiting for them occupied the entire floor. The two goons stayed behind, one on each side of the door to the suite. They appeared to be already familiar with the protocol. Jessica took in all of the splendor before her when they entered. The ceiling was so high up that she was sure they could fit an entire house in there.

She dove onto the leather couch, letting all of her muscles relax. Roca went straight to the bar. He grabbed a bottle of vodka that could easily cost between two and three hundred dollars and poured two glasses. At least, he wasn't the type to rush into things; she appreciated that.

Jessica sat up and waited for him to come back. He put her glass in front of her on the coffee table and sat next to her, flashing a smile. She took the glass and brought it to her lips. She stopped, thinking that it'd be better if she had all of her senses intact for the mission. Now, what was left was figuring out how to get the info out of him.

"C'mon, babe, take a sip," he said, his smile seeming forced.

"You know," said Jessica, trying to change the subject. "I think I've seen you somewhere. Are you some kinda celebrity?"

Roca's smile now seemed genuine. "Well, I wouldn't say a celebrity. I'm more of a local figure."

"No wonder." His eyes wandered between the glass and her. Her gut told her that it was best not to take even a sip of it. She placed her glass back on the table. "So, tell me a bit more about yourself. What makes you so popular?"

"I told you before on the way here."

I wasn't listening.

"Well, yeah, but I mean, I want you to tell me a little more. I love a man with power."

He looked down. For a split second, she saw a hint of frustration on Roca's face, but it was replaced by a bright smile almost immediately. "Let's make a toast first. To break the ice, you know? You seem a little tense."

Maybe because you keep insisting on me to drink.

He grabbed the glass from the table and gave it to her. Jessica reluctantly took it. They clinked the glasses.

"*Salud,*" he said and chugged the drink down in one gulp.

She put the glass on her lips and raised her head back. Her lips sealed shut. She swallowed her own saliva and pretended to frown. "Now, this is some good stuff."

Roca's happy demeanor disappeared almost immediately. His expression soured.

"Bullshit," he spat. "You didn't drink any of it."

She recoiled in surprise. "W-What? Of course, I did. I just didn't drink as much as you did."

He leaned in, his eyes on fire. "Then, you woulda realized it wasn't vodka."

Jessica's heart sank. She brought the glass a bit closer and sniffed it. There was no trace of alcohol.

It's water!

Before she could react, he lunged at her. In less than a second, she was immobilized. He climbed on top of her with his left hand over her mouth, muffling her screams for help. The glass fell and spilled the spiked water over the carpet. Roca pulled a gun out of his pants.

Shit! What the fuck?

She fought instinctively, kicking and scratching as much as she could. But the second she saw the 9mm, her whole body paralyzed.

"That's better," he whispered. "I like them quiet and submissive."

She jerked her head sideways as tears slid down her face to the couch. Most people didn't feel true fear during the entirety of their lives. She, on the other hand, had had many moments in her life that had been truly terrifying. And being restrained by a gorilla with a handgun, with the choice of letting herself get raped or killed was definitely on the top five.

Roca lowered the 9mm until the muzzle of the gun touched her temple.

"If you scream . . ." he said.

She nodded frantically. Roca removed his hand from Jessica's mouth, and she took in a deep breath of fresh air.

"Please . . ." she whispered between gasps. "I won't charge you . . . we can talk this through…"

"You think this is about money, you stupid bitch?" he asked with disdain. "Look around you! I can afford whatever the fuck I please."

"So this is just some sick power fantasy?" she asked, unable to contain the words from leaving her mouth.

He didn't take the comment too fondly. "You say one more word, and I'll blow your fucking brains out, right here. Do you think I'll hesitate? You think anybody's gonna care about some dead whore?"

Roca snatched a tissue out of his pocket and stuffed it in her mouth. Whatever that tissue was used for, she didn't want to know. The smell and the taste on her tongue were repulsive. Tears filled her eyes as her gag reflex kicked in, and she tried to fight it off, refusing to die choked by her own vomit.

Jessica started to kick, her legs barely twisting and struggling under Roca. Her hands went to his face, trying to scratch him. Roca grabbed both her hands with one hand and locked them up above her while he unlocked his belt and began to pull down his pants, gun still in hand.

"You're only making it harder," he said, the foul smell of his breath hitting her. "It won't hurt if you stay still."

Fuck that!

Her left hand broke free. She patted the carpet, desperately searching for something, anything that she could use against her attacker. Her fingers slid across a smooth surface. The glass she had was still intact. She grabbed it and smashed it in his cheek. She closed her eyes as a rain of small pieces of glass and blood poured on her. He staggered and tried to cover the wound. She took the opportunity and pushed him off her. The fat pervert fell to the side, crashing on the carpet and knocking over the coffee table.

Like lightning, she shot up. The gun had fallen off to the side. She lunged at it and snatched it off the floor. She pointed the 9mm toward Roca, who was still trying to get up. The right side of his face was covered in red, his pants halfway down to his knees.

Roca froze, his eyes locked on her. The expression on his face was that of pure hatred. Jessica spat out the tissue.

"If you scream," Jessica warned. "I won't think twice to pull the trigger."

She was bluffing, of course. She was holding the gun with both hands, shaking and cold sweat dripping off her back. She couldn't imagine taking a life. But if it came to it and it was time to decide who was going to live through the night, she was willing to bet on herself.

"Listen, you little bitch—"

"Shut up, fatass. I'm not here to suck on your micro dick. I need you to tell me something."

"I won't tell you shit!" he shouted.

She lowered the gun to his groin. "Are you sure about that?"

Roca's face paled. For the first time in the whole night, he looked afraid.

"You shoot, and they'll come right in and blow your head off!"

"And you'll be dickless for the rest of your life. I'll make sure there's nothing left to salvage your little sack of meat."

Somebody knocked at the door. A muffled voice came from the other side.

"Is everything okay, boss?"

Jessica started to moan, quietly at first, but then louder and louder, as if she were following a rhythm only she could hear. She saw the shadow from the gap underneath the door disappear and stopped. Roca looked at the gun and then right back at her. "What do you want?"

Jessica was still trying to catch her breath. She waited for a second, lingering his suffering a little longer before asking. "Where's Los Santos' hideout?"

Roca recoiled in surprise. A half grin turned into a full smile, then into laughter.

"Are you fucking serious?"

"Serious enough to blow your nuts off."

He stopped laughing. "Who sent you? Nicholai? He's paranoid. None of us is trying to fuck him over."

"It doesn't matter who sent me." She didn't even know herself. From the looks of it, it seemed to be a gang war kind of thing. What she couldn't decipher was why she'd been chosen to do the dirty work. "You know what I'm talking about, and I'm going to get out of here with an answer from you. And whether you leave with a dick or a lump between your legs depends on you."

Roca took a deep breath. "Look, I'm not going to fuck over Nicholai. We've been together in this business for years. But, I heard a rumor. That's all that is, a rumor. They've been saying that the Los Santos have been hanging out on a farm near Marty's Casino. That's all I know, I swear. I didn't tell Nicholai because . . ."

"I don't give a fuck," said Jessica, sharp as a knife.

She pulled out her phone and texted the info to NV, a few grammatical errors along the way, but that's what writing with her left hand while holding a gun with the other would do. It took mere seconds for her to receive a message back.

Do you think he's telling the truth?

Jessica shrugged and replied.

Have him at gunpoint. I don't think he's lying.

Then, it occurred to her. Maybe this asshole was the key to find out who was blackmailing her.

"When you asked if Nicholai sent me, who do you mean exactly?"

Roca squinted, confused. "Nicholai Vines. He's the one who sent you, right?"

"Vines?" she asked. "The club's owner?"

"Of course, you stupid bitch, who else would I be talking about?"

Her phone beeped. *Not the method I thought you'd use*, NV wrote. *But it got the job done. Congratulations, you've passed your first trial.*

First trial? She tried to text back, but the message bounced. She then got a notification that the number she was trying to reach was unavailable.

"Fuck!" she shouted.

"I told you, it was just a stupid rumor," Roca spat.

"You've served your purpose," said Jessica.

She stepped toward him and struck him with the butt of the gun where the blood was leaking from. Roca fell limp to the side. The bastard was unconscious before he hit the ground.

Jessica stepped over him, grabbed her stuff, and put the gun in her purse. On her way out, she made sure to wink at the bodyguards.

"Your boss is a beast," Jessica said.

She then giggled like a schoolgirl and walked to the elevator. Before the doors closed, she heard one of the guards whisper to the other. "She seems to like it rough."

Yeah, I do, she thought on her way down.

And things were only going to get rougher.

SLOTH

Oliver checked his watch for the tenth time in the last five minutes. He had been told to park close to a construction site where a new mall was supposed to open in a year or two. For now, it was just the skeleton of a building, with sand and dust sweeping across the abandoned street.

He took a deep drag on his joint as he scratched his neck. The high was starting to kick in. It had never felt like the first time, back when he could feel as if his entire body floated in a cloud and all the colors around him had taken a whole new level of sharpness. Now, it was nothing more than a way to relax, a little help to sleep every once in a while.

Oliver snuck what was left of it back in his pocket and crossed his arms. The air was cold and dry that night. He scanned the place, unsure of what to expect. NV had said nothing. Neither who was coming to meet him nor what that person looked like or exactly what they should do. Oliver had only been told to take the car he'd stolen to that location and wait for someone. It had been more than twenty minutes past the agreed time, and Oliver was afraid that if he tried to leave or contact NV, he'd fail the trial. Maybe it was some kind of test.

It's not like I have better shit to do.

His concern increased a thousandfold when he saw some movement in between the bushes on the other side of the parking lot.

Oliver straightened up, his heart throbbing. A shadow materialized from the darkness. The silhouette of a man was bathed in the streetlamp light. The man had a hoodie covering his face. He carried over his shoulder what looked to be a shotgun, two rifles, one on each hand, and a backpack that seemed to be dragging him down as if it was full of rocks.

The man strode to him, and Oliver felt his legs shaking, tempted to jump back to the car and get the fuck outta there. He remained still, however, his head held high. The hooded man stopped a few steps away from him. Oliver could now see his scruff, grey beard, tired eyes, and dry skin. The man exhaled deeply. He dropped the rifles on the floor, exhausted.

"You okay, dude?" Oliver asked, trying to hide the fact he was about to piss himself.

The hooded man took off his backpack and dropped it. He got down on one knee and looked up. "Do I look okay?"

"You look like shit." If Oliver had one good attribute, it was that he could be brutally honest.

The man chuckled. "Could you help this old man out?"

Oliver grabbed the bag and felt his shoulder muscles straining as he lifted it. He basically dragged it to the trunk of the car. The man got back to his feet and grabbed the two rifles. Oliver did his best to fit the weapons inside the trunk. He closed it and landed his eyes on the man beside him.

"Now what?"

"We leave the car here," the man said.

"What? Really?"

The man shrugged. "That's what he said."

"After all this shit? We just leave the car and the weapons in the middle of nowhere?"

"Kid, the less you know, the better. It's worked for me so far."

Oliver ran his hand over his head. The man turned around and started to walk away.

"Where are you going?" Oliver asked.

The man waved his hand without turning back. "Home."

This guy had to know something about this whole situation and how fucked up it was. Oliver didn't want to try his luck and get shot for asking too many questions, but his lips moved on their own.

"Why are you doing this?"

This time, the hooded man looked over his shoulder.

"'Cause I'm greedy."

GLUTTONY

Matt had to cancel his date, but now he had another. After hiding the sickening display in his yard, he called Oswaldo and told him that they would have to postpone their meeting. Oswaldo did not take it very well. Even so, Matt assumed that there were always more fish in the sea, even if not all of them were willing to jump from the sea straight to the fryer.

Matt parked just a block away from the bar where his prey should be. The name was Brian Thompson, a drunken mess of a human being who spent his rent money on booze. It wouldn't be difficult prey. It was just a matter of isolating and attacking, as he had done with so many women. With men, Matt had a different strategy, a more subtle one since it was trickier to subdue a man. However, he couldn't pretend to be homosexual this time to attract his prey, so brute force was not out of the question.

Matt turned off the engine and waited in the dark, his eyes locked on the bar's entrance. It was almost closing time; he just needed to stay there a bit longer. Patience wasn't a virtue; it was a skill, one he had learned to master over the years.

Finally, an old man staggered out of the bar. The man wore a buttoned-down shirt and saggy mismatched pants. Matt double-checked the picture on his phone. It was him, no doubt about it. He looked around his car for the etorphine, a highly effective sedative that could immobilize even the strongest man in a matter of seconds. He had managed to get a load of the stuff without raising an eyebrow, thanks to a contact in the hospital he worked in.

Matt skillfully filled the hypodermic needle with the substance, glancing up at the drunken man walking away from him. NV knew his route, and Matt had seen in the GPS that Brian would have to walk through an alleyway on his way home. That would be the perfect chance.

Matt clenched the needle, hiding it in his arm and tugging it into his jacket's pocket. He stepped down from the car and walked briskly to where Brian had gone. The tip of his tongue slid through his lips, almost salivating, like a hungry hound with its eyes locked on dinner.

Brian stumbled to the side, his hand running through the wall as he took a turn to the left.

It's time.

Brian stopped on a corner and brought his hands to his crotch, ready to open the zipper but struggling. By the time Brian realized something was wrong, the hypodermic needle was already deep inside the tender skin of his neck. The liquid entered quickly and precisely through the aorta. Brian turned around, disoriented, with his zipper open and the belt undone. He tried to hit Matt with a hook but instead fell to the ground ungraciously.

Matt took a last look around him, knelt down, and grabbed the guy's armpit. He put the man's unconscious body over his right shoulder and rose to his feet as if Brian was nothing more than a bag of dirty clothes.

Matt left the alley and met eyes with two girls laughing. Until a second ago, they had been focused on their own conversation, but their faces turned grim when they saw him. Matt just smiled.

"My brother had one drink too many. He told me he wouldn't drink like this anymore, and this is what I get for believing him."

One of the girls chuckled and went on her way. The other one followed her friend nervously, stealing glances over her shoulder. Surely, she suspected something, but nothing concrete and their demeanor showed that they were also a little tipsy, so surely they would not even remember their small encounter.

With some difficulty, Matthew managed to place Brian in the passenger seat. He put on Brian's belt and then sat on the driver's side. Putting Brian in the trunk may raise too many questions if a cop pulled him over and decided to take a look at his car. He'd never been that unlucky, but it was better to be prepared. This way, he could pretend to be his friend's designated driver taking him home. After all, Brian should stay in the dream world for at least a couple of hours.

Matt arrived at his house, parked in his garage, and dragged Brian out with ease. His assignment had been a breeze. A little outside of his comfort zone but otherwise dull compared to some stuff he'd done on his own accord. The shoulder he was carrying Brian on was aching now. He decided to put Brian on the floor and drag him down the rest of the way.

The process of tying Brian up in a chair in his basement turned out to be cumbersome. But after finishing up and sending the picture of his hard work to NV, he couldn't help to feel a rewarding sense of accomplishment.

The phone beeped.

Good. Now I need you to beat the living shit out of him. Don't kill him. Send video and pics.

Matt read the message again, incredulous about what was happening. He shrugged and cracked his neck. A smile drew wide on his face.

"If life gives you lemons . . ."

WRATH

Trevor clenched his fists, the veins in his arms bulging as if about to explode. His blood had been boiling just a few minutes ago when some asshole decided to cut in line in front of him in the supermarket. Trevor sucker-punched that fool in the face. The asshole deserved it, but all the people around them did not agree. They glared at Trevor with judging eyes as if he was some monster. Hypocrites, all of them. They caused a commotion that got Trevor kicked out of the supermarket. Now he was walking the streets empty-handed, with no other option than to go to another supermarket.

Trevor looked down at his knuckles. They were red and throbbing, with dry, dark red stains. What a waste of time. He reached the intersection and pressed the crosswalk button. As he waited for the light to turn, his phone vibrated in his back pocket.

"Now what?" Trevor barked.

It was a message from an unknown number. It happened often. For some reason, his phone company had decided to give him a magnet of scammers and spammers instead of a proper phone line.

This one, however, was the first one to have a file attached to it. A video. With all the social media craze, advertisements had gotten sneakier by the day. He decided to check the text and tell them to fuck off. Most of them didn't allow for replies, but it was still a satisfying thing to do.

He opened it, and his jaw dropped as he read it.

Hello Wrath.

You don't know me, but I know you. You haven't been the same since the accident. You've let your life be consumed by hatred. You're a ticking bomb waiting to go off at any moment. So now I'm offering you a chance to release that pain in a wonderful explosion of rage. Do as I say, and I'll make sure you meet face to face with the bastard who took your family.

Still dumbfounded, Trevor tapped on the video. He had to put his hand over the screen to cover the sun's reflection to properly see what was going on. It was shot in some dark, musty basement. In the middle of it was some dude tied to a chair, covered in blood, his clothes ripped and torn.

Whoever was filming the man panned over around the chair, covering every angle. They seemed to enjoy what they were doing. Trevor thought this had to be some sort of fucked up prank. But when the camera guy zoomed in on the man's swollen face, Trevor recognized him instantly.

It was Brian Thompson. The drunk driver who had slammed his car against Trevor's, killing his wife and daughter in the process. The man had survived unscathed, and not only that, but the fucking bastard had been called to trial for manslaughter, and the charges were overturned on a technicality.

The video ended. The pedestrian light turned green. People walked by him as they crossed the street. Trevor stood still, his eyes glued to the screen.

He ran his hand over his bald head, trying to make sense of the situation he was in. Trevor wasn't sure what was creepier, that someone had kidnapped and tortured the man who had ruined Trevor's life, or that he was seriously considering accepting the proposal.

His mind kept racing, thinking about how crazy the whole situation was, but his thumbs were already tapping on the digital keyboard, asking for instructions on what he needed to do.

PRIDE

The night before had been a nightmare. Tim had not been able to close his eyes since. He spent hours reflecting on who could be behind this charade.

His mind wandered. He had been on the verge of a mental breakdown a couple of times throughout the night but had managed to maintain his composure.

It wasn't until he saw the sunrise from the window of his kitchen that he realized how much time had passed.

At 6 a.m., he had to take a shower, change his clothes, and go to work like any other day. Tim felt the judging gaze of his employees. Each and every one of them suspecting the horrible crime that threatened to ruin his life. Timothy spent all morning working, his exhausted body screaming, and his eyes growing heavier.

He decided to leave early. After giving it a lot of thought, there was only one person he could confront about it.

Tim exited the office building in long strides. He reached for his phone and called the number he had hidden under the contact name "Joe Office." The line rang for several minutes until he was sent straight to the voicemail again.

"Dammit!" he cursed as he shoved the phone back in his pocket.

Jessica wasn't picking up. He texted her asking to meet in a different place than usual. He'd sent her the address and asked her to be there as soon as possible.

The place was only a few blocks away from his office. A discreet little motel cramped on a blind street. He had been tempted to go there before but had decided to avoid it due to how close it was to his office. At two o'clock in the afternoon, right after the lunch break, he was sure he wouldn't find any familiar faces around, so he decided to take a chance.

Once in the motel's lobby, he paid for a room and texted her the room number. After an excruciating fifteen minutes of uncertainty, she finally replied.

Someone's eager ;) Sorry hun, but it'll have to wait. I'm solving some personal issues right now.

Tim hit the call button one more time. Now that he knew she had her phone in hand, there was no excuse not to pick up.

"Hello?" her voice was soft like silk.

"Jess! I need to see you. Face to face. It's urgent."

"Look, Tim, I don't like turning you down, but . . ."

"No, Jessica, you don't understand! Someone's blackmailing me. They found out about us. They must've hacked me or something. Hell, they could be listening to this conversation right now!"

There was silence on the other side of the line.

"Hello?" Tim called. "Are you still there?"

"I'll be there in twenty."

She hung up. Tim stood vigilant, his eyes glancing at the clock every two minutes. He'd never been the anxious type; he was used to having everything under control. In the last few years, all it took for him to get anything he wanted was to say it out loud and open his wallet. In the situation he was in, however, there was nothing he could do that wouldn't potentially dig him deeper into a hole where he'd end up broke, in jail, or maybe even dead.

Tim shook those thoughts from his head. He wasn't going to die or get arrested. Worst-case scenario, he would be exposed for cheating on his wife.

But you've already crossed that line, haven't you? he thought. *The moment you dropped a corpse on someone's backyard.*

Tim felt light-headed. None of this should be happening. None of it. He'd made mistakes, but he wasn't a bad man. He didn't deserve any of this shit. Tim's hands went to his scalp, his fingers tightening on his hair. He almost ripped his hair off at the sound of a loud knocking on the door. He jolted and lunged at it.

Just as he turned the knob, Jessica barged in, pushing him to the side. It was weird to see her like this. Not only was she wearing regular clothes and no makeup, but she also looked like she'd been run over by a truck. Tim's head jerked back in surprise, wondering if she too had been digging up bodies in the middle of the desert.

"Who's blackmailing you?" she asked bluntly.

"I don't know. It's the reason I called you. I figured if somebody knew anything, it'd be you."

Jessica shrugged as her eyes wandered around the murky room.

"Well, I don't. What do they want? Money?"

Tim's mind manifested the creepy image of the body he'd carried the night before; the bones buried deep in the sand, rotten.

"No. It's definitely not money they want."

"What then?"

"It's like . . . a game to them. They want to control you. Make you do stuff you despise for the hell of it. Or maybe there's a plan in motion. One I can't see."

Jessica's eyes grew wider. She opened her mouth and closed it again. Her lips trembled, hesitant.

"The person who's harassing you. Do they have some sort of number or name they're texting you from?"

"Private number. Tried calling, but the operator said it wasn't available. Whoever is doing this is very tech-savvy. The only way I know it's them is because it comes with a signature. Some sort of anagram. NV."

Just like that, Jessica's tanned skin turned pale. Her breathing seemed to stop altogether. Tim stepped closer to her.

"Jess, do you know who I'm talking about?" She remained still like a statue. He grabbed her by the shoulders and shook her. "Jess!"

She jolted back to reality, startled. Her expression was one Tim had never seen before from her. He was used to her seductive, sarcastic, and playful nature, a femme fatale willing to turn his boring life around. But the woman he was holding wasn't the one he knew; he was holding a little girl, petrified and scared.

"I-I'm being harassed by the same person," she finally confessed at the verge of tears.

"Shit," Tim let out as he released her.

"It has to be someone we both know," she said.

"Not necessarily, I mean, any skilled hacker could access your info remotely, right? Without ever having to interact with you."

"Yes, but don't you think this is a bit personal? I mean, they're not asking us for money or retaliation. I don't know what they asked you to do, but I was sent on some kind of mission. It's like you said, it's like a game. And it's not just an internet troll. This is some serious shit, involving shady people."

"What do you mean?"

Jessica shrugged, avoiding his gaze. "I'm sorry, but I'm not telling you more than what you need to know."

"Do you want to find who's responsible for this or not?"

She stayed quiet as she turned around and walked aimlessly around the room.

"Do you know somebody involved in drugs or cartels?" she asked. "Any sort of shady business, really."

Tim shrugged.

"I know a couple of people who are under investigation and others who are . . . well, let's just say, have shaken a few hands that shouldn't be shaken."

"Any names come to mind?" she asked as she turned back at him, biting her nails.

"Julian Chavodski. Luis Roca. James West. Nicholai Vines . . ."

"Nicholai Vines?" she interrupted. "I know Luis Roca, and trust me, he isn't the one we're looking for. But there's one person who would have benefited from what I did last night. Nicholai Vines."

"Really?" Tim's hands went to his waist. "I mean, he owns a few businesses around the city. One of his restaurants was under investigation for being a front for money laundering, but nothing came out of it from what I've heard. The guy seems clean."

"A few bribes can go a long way," she pointed out.

"If his influence is that high, I'm pretty sure someone would know something about it."

"I know a guy." Her face seemed to brighten up. "A dealer. He's a regular. Maybe he's got something on Vines."

"I could make a few calls and talk to Vines myself."

Jessica's head jerked back in surprise.

"You actually want to talk to him directly?"

"I'm a good judge of character," Tim explained. "I've met Vines a couple of times before, and despite his charm, there's always been something off about him. I'm pretty sure that if I can talk to him face-to-face, I'd be able to see if he's the one messing around with us."

"Then make your calls, and I'll make mine. If we're both alive by tomorrow, we'll meet again and discuss what we found."

"Sounds like a plan."

"A terrible plan. But it's the only one we got."

WRATH

Dusk was quickly approaching. Elongated shadows gave the construction site an eerie facade. Trevor walked around the compound, vigilant to find the car he was told would be there. He circled the structure, careful not to meet a worker or a pedestrian who could be loitering nearby.

He finally caught a glance of a vehicle awkwardly parked to the side of the building, hiding in the building's shadow. Trevor's pulse quickened as he stepped closer and opened the trunk.

He licked his lips, slowly revealing the small arsenal hidden inside. There was a bag, a shotgun, and two rifles. His instructions had been clear: Go to the construction site, take the car to the designated address, and "kill them all."

Trevor drove for what felt like hours, taking the fastest route out of town and into the desert. There had been nothing but darkness for miles around. It was as if the road manifested in front of him from some black dimension. Only the roar of the engine accompanied the sepulchral silence. It wasn't until well into the night that the GPS of the car startled him.

"In half a mile, turn right," announced the female voice coming from the device.

Trevor swore under his breath and did as he was told. He turned off the engine and was promptly submerged in the night.

In the distance, to the west, he could see a spot of light. It was property, a huge house that seemed to serve as some kind of farm. Who would've thought there were people living so far out in the desert and with a farm in the middle of such a barren land.

He put one rifle over his shoulder, the 9mm on his hip, and grabbed the shotgun. Two belts covered his torso with pouches filled with ammo. Trevor clenched the cold metal. It had been so long since the last time he'd held a proper weapon between his fingers with the intention of using it on another human being.

Back when he was a soldier, he dreaded the feeling, but he grew fonder of it with each death to his name. He had denied it to everyone and even to himself until the night his wife and daughter died. Since then, he had craved the feeling of the stiff pump of a gun on his shoulder and the loud bang after pulling the trigger, effectively ending somebody's life and perpetuating his own.

It was like a dream, one he didn't want to wake up from. Trevor glided over the now cold sand of the desert. His heavy boots were as quiet as the wind. He was like a ghost.

Trevor crept until he was close enough to see the inside of the house from the windows. The bedroom had the curtains drawn, but he could perfectly see a couple of silhouettes. On the first floor, three men sat on a stained couch facing an old TV in the living room. One of them was tying up his left arm to then inject a needle well into his forearm. His eyes rolled back to his skull as his head fell back to the couch. Another one was smoking. Trevor figured it wasn't tobacco. The third one just lay on the couch, his eyes glued to the TV screen.

Just a bunch of junkies, Trevor thought. *Just like the drunk sonofabitch that took my life away.*

Trevor let the fear fade away. Through his veins, blood boiled, bringing a feeling that most people tried to evade, but one he welcomed with open arms. He let out a grunt in the silent night before continuing on his path. He was going to receive the morning soaked in blood. Either his or someone else's.

He knocked on the front door and waited. Someone from inside shouted in excitement.

"Pizza's here!"

"Shut the fuck up, Greg," yelled another. "Nobody ordered no pizza."

Trevor stood in his power position. The muzzle of the shotgun pointing at the center of the door. The knob turned.

"Look, man," said a man while opening the front door. "If you're gonna come talking about Jesus and sh—"

His words stopped, and his jaw dropped at the sight of the shotgun. Trevor didn't give him time to scream for help. He pulled the trigger. His shoulder pushed back in an explosive thrust as the night lit up. The man's torso blew up in a crimson display as he staggered back a few steps. A look of wild disbelief and desperation filled the junkie's eyes as he dropped to the wooden floor.

Trevor stepped over the still-contorting body as he scanned the place. Another man came rushing through the entrance leading to the living room. His pale and scrawny figure stopped short once he saw Trevor standing over his dead friend. The man spun around to flee, but Trevor had already taken a shot at him. Half of the man's shoulder turned into a red lump of flesh. The man screamed in pain as his legs gave up, and he fell to his knees.

Trevor put the shotgun on the back of the man's head.

"P-Please, dude," the man begged. "We'll give you anything. We have cash. We have drugs, anything. Please, just let me go."

"I'm sorry, bud." Trevor wasn't sorry in the slightest. "There's somebody I need to meet, and if I have to burn the whole city to the ground to see him, then I'll do it."

Before the man could utter another word, Trevor blew his brains out.

A sharp pain pierced through Trevor's shoulder, dangerously close to his neck. He staggered and let out a grunt as he turned around and grabbed the scissors that were sticking into him. His gaze met with a woman's. She was naked except for a black robe barely covering her. Her mascara had run down her face, covered in tears and sweat.

"Sneaky bitch," he gasped, a smirk peeking on his lips.

Trevor pulled the scissors out of his skin. The wound gushed out blood rhythmically, in sync with his heartbeat. She had tried to stab him in the neck.

"If only you were a little taller," Trevor said as he let out a chuckle.

The woman stood still. She lunged at him, her hand squeezing on his wound as they both dropped to the floor. She fell on him. The shotgun sprang out of Trevor's fingers. With animalistic grunts and screams, she began to press Trevor's wounded shoulder. He screamed in pain, grabbed her hips, and pushed her aside as if she were a rag doll.

The woman's back collided with the cold metal of the shotgun. In a swift movement, she picked up the shotgun and aimed it at her attacker while rising to her feet. In turn, Trevor removed the 9mm from his waist, the muzzle pointing directly at the woman's forehead. Both stood petrified, expectant of each other's movement.

Trevor's hand trembled, not out of fear but from accumulated anger. How dare that bitch attack him like that? Who did she think she was? She could have fled through the front door without Trevor noticing but still decided to attack him. He could see in her gaze that the girl was deranged, probably drugged out of her mind.

"You better not do anything stupid, honey," Trevor said, his voice sharp. His whole body felt on fire. "I'm already pissed off. You don't want to make it worse."

The girl's gaze shook sporadically between him, the gun, and the stairs she had come down from. It was then he understood. She was protecting someone.

"Oh," he said. "You got a boyfriend upstairs, don't you?"

Her eyes widened to the point of looking like a scared fish.

"That's so sweet of you. To try and protect him. It's a shame you can't."

The woman gripped the shotgun tightly, her finger lingering on the trigger. Trevor shot first. The woman's head jerked back as a red spot appeared in between her eyebrows. The shotgun dropped heavily on the wooden floor, followed by the woman's body.

Trevor kicked her aside and grabbed the shotgun. He crept up the stairs. There were only two rooms. Without wasting any more time, Trevor kicked open one of the doors.

Nothing but a few stained mattresses. There was another room at the end of the hall. He walked toward it. His hands were sticky with blood and sweat, mixed with the fresh smell of gunpowder. It was exhilarating. He slammed his good shoulder on the door, which swung open and bounced back.

Only one bed. A shirtless, tattooed man lay on it like a starfish. His snorting was monstrous, seemingly able to shake the whole room. Trevor wondered what he must have taken to not be awoken by the sound of a shotgun being fired repeatedly. He shrugged.

"At least he'll die peacefully."

He pulled the trigger. The man's snorting was interrupted by the blast as his head got obliterated. Trevor dropped the shotgun and took a deep breath. He wiped the blood off his pants and pulled out his phone. He took one picture of each corpse. The flash of the light gave them an eerie shiny reflection to all the gore as if it was part of a display in a museum. Trevor's stomach turned a bit, but he ignored it. He had learned to figuratively look the other way a long time ago. He sent the images to NV and asked:

Is that all of them?

NV replied in just a few seconds.

Yes. Now finish the job, and you'll be rewarded.

Trevor put the phone back in his pocket. He went to the basement. Just like NV had said, the whole place had been turned into some sort of improvised meth lab. A door leading to the garage swung open, inviting him. The wind gushed through, shaking the place in an erratic rhythm. There were four gasoline canisters resting in a corner. Trevor followed his instincts, no longer thinking of the ramifications of his actions.

He poured the gasoline all over the house, not missing one room. When one canister emptied, he'd go for the next one until there wasn't a single drop left.

Trevor stood at the entrance of the house as he tossed the last canister to the side. He lit a match and dropped it to his feet, where a trail of gasoline led to the living room. A blue haze ran up the trail, lighting the night.

Trevor walked backward for a few feet as he watched in awe of the spectacle. In just a matter of seconds, the whole house had been engulfed in flames. The smell of burnt wood and flesh filled his lungs as he headed back to his car.

SLOTH

The cold tiles of the bathroom made contact with Oliver's bare knees as he knelt in front of the bathtub. He was only wearing shorts and an old T-shirt, just in case his cousin Freddy splashed water onto him. Freddy laid inside the tub, barely submerged in the warm water, clinging to the wheelchair beside it.

"C'mon, Freddy," Oliver begged. "Nobody likes to take baths. But if you don't, you'll be filthy, and auntie Ana will be really pissed with both of us. Do you want to test that woman's patience?"

Freddy's grip on the chair loosened. Oliver grabbed him under the armpits and lifted him easily. Despite his skinny build, Oliver was perfectly capable of carrying his cousin. After all, the poor boy was pure bone. Freddy's disability didn't allow him to move much of his body, and he'd lost his speech over the years. Thank God the boy was smart and had managed to find a program on the Internet to communicate on his computer. Otherwise, he would've had a rough time speaking his mind since his motor skills had gone to shit, so anything small like writing on a piece of paper had become a challenging task.

Unfortunately, neither the laptop nor any electrical devices were allowed during bath time, so Freddy could only communicate in the forms of gestures and nods for the time being.

"So, how's your day been?" Oliver asked as he scrubbed with a sponge on Freddy's chest.

Freddy lowered his gaze in a gentle nod.

"Good," Oliver replied with a smile. "No pain?"

Freddy jerked his head from side to side; the movement was so subtle it was barely noticeable.

"Those new pills the doctor gave you. They're the real deal, huh?"

Freddy displayed a weak smile. The occasions when Oliver saw his cousin smile were few and far between.

There was a knock on the front door. Oliver stopped for a second and tilted his head. They knocked again. It was definitely from their house. Oliver let out a sigh.

"Probably some salesman," he said as he stood up. "Stay here."

Freddy rolled his eyes. It took Oliver a second to realize the stupidity of what he had said.

"I'm sorry. You know what I mean. I'll be right back."

Oliver went down the stairs. The knocking turned louder.

"Alright, I'm coming!" he yelled. "Jesus, look, man, whatever you're selling, I ain't buying . . ." He opened the door to find a beautiful woman standing on the other side. He recognized her instantly. "Alright, maybe I am."

Jessica barged in and pushed him aside. She took a quick glance at the street behind her before closing the door. Oliver stood bewildered as he eyed her up and down.

It was Jessica, one of the best escorts in town. Definitely one of Oliver's favorites, but one that he had only been able to afford a few times. Although her rates were high, she was worth it. Now she was standing in his living room as if she had a door-to-door service. Oliver wondered if he had called her while high.

"D-Did I call you? Because if I did, I'm sorry. I don't have enough cash. I don't know what I must've been thinking . . ."

"You didn't call me," she said. She looked altered. Now that Oliver took a closer look at her, he noticed that she wasn't wearing her regular attire. She was there with regular street clothes and absented from the sexy aura that used to surround her. "I need a favor."

"You need some dope? I figured a woman like you could get all the dope in the world. Hell, I bet you could get it for free."

Jessica frowned as she crossed her arms. "No. I don't need dope. I need you to tell me who's your supplier."

"My what?"

"Who gives you the drug?"

"I know whatcha mean, but I'm not telling you. I ain't no snitch. Besides, do you have any idea the trouble I'd be in?"

She let out a sigh. "I promise this won't get back to you. I just . . . I got into a lot of trouble, and I need to talk to Nicholai Vines."

Oliver's eyes widened, he put a finger on his lips, and his voice lowered to a whisper as if somebody could be listening to their conversation.

"Whoa, whoa. Chill out, girl. That guy is too high up the ladder. What kind of mess did you get yourself into?" He raised his hands in defeat. "You know, actually, I don't want to know. So, could you please leave?"

A dry bump echoed from the top of the stairs. Oliver cursed under his breath. He climbed the stairs skipping steps. Jessica followed.

They reached the middle of the hall on the second floor. A pool of water was expanding from one of the bathrooms. Oliver skipped over the water and pushed the door ajar. His cousin Freddy had half of his body outside the tub. Soaps and a couple of bottles of shampoo were scattered on the floor.

"Freddy, c'mon, dude, what the fuck." Oliver knelt, avoiding slipping in the water. Jessica stayed at the bathroom door.

Oliver got Freddy back in position in the tub. "I told you I'd be back. You don't have to be so impatient." Oliver turned over his shoulder, surprised to see Jessica had followed him all the way there. "I guess you remember my cousin."

Jessica stared at Freddy. She struggled to force a smile. "How could I forget? He was one of my favorite clients."

Freddy seemed surprised to see her there, if not a little uncomfortable. Oliver couldn't blame him, it had been a while since he took his cousin to lose his virginity to Jessica, but the situation they were in was far from flattering.

"You made him real happy, you know?" Oliver confessed while putting the shampoo bottles back in their place. "After that night, he kept begging me to take him back to you." Freddy shot him a murderous look. "But I didn't have the money for it, and hell, you're an expensive one."

"Nothing good comes for cheap," she said with a more genuine smile.

"I guess not."

Jessica brushed her hair behind her ear. "But, I could give you guys a freebie if you help me."

"Hell, no!" Oliver spat. "You think I'm sticking my neck out just so I can get laid? I'm sorry, Jess. You're great and all, but no pussy is worth dying for."

Oliver stood up, grabbed a towel, and threw it to the ground, using his feet to scrub the floor.

"This won't get back to you, I promise."

"How can you know that? These people are dangerous, you know. They can find a rat if they get their minds to it, and don't get me wrong, but you seem the type to spill their beans quickly."

Jessica arched an eyebrow and crossed her arms. "You'd be surprised."

"I bet."

"Look," Jessica snapped. "I wouldn't be asking this if it wasn't an emergency. Someone has been threatening me, stalking me, making my life miserable, and if I don't do anything, shit is going to get worse."

Oliver stopped scrubbing the floor and raised his head. Jessica's eyes were watery. He could tell she was making a tremendous effort to hold herself together. He had to ask.

"Who's threatening you?"

"I don't know," she said, a lone tear finally making its way down her cheek. She wasn't trying to make him feel bad; he was an expert in seeing through shit like that. They weren't tears of sadness or even fear. They were born from anger. "But whoever's doing it is about to ruin my life. So I plan to stop him before it gets to that."

Oliver couldn't help but relate to that. The world around him seemed like a nightmare he couldn't wake up from. Ever since that night, he had been looking over his shoulder, afraid that someone would be stalking him or the next text from that psycho hacker.

He opened his mouth to say something but was cut off by a wheezing to his side. Freddy was now gesturing to Oliver, the boy's chest going up and down in a frenzy.

"Oh, shit!" Oliver stormed out of the bathroom, almost slipping on his way to his cousin's bedroom.

"What's going on?" Jessica asked, unsure of how to react. "Is he okay?"

"No!" Oliver exclaimed as he grabbed the oxygen tank and mask and rushed back.

He rolled the tank inside the bathroom and quickly but gently put on the mask on his cousin's face. Freddy laid back in relief as he took deep puffs of air.

"His condition gives him a hard time with his lungs," Oliver said, trying to catch his breath. "He sometimes struggles to breathe, so it was lucky that the hospital lent him a few of these."

"I see."

Oliver swallowed, struggling to keep his mouth shut. "So, how do you know Vines is the guy you're looking for?"

"I don't, but it's the only lead I have. Whoever's messaging me has the acronym N and V as a signature." She shrugged. "It seems like one hell of a coincidence."

The letters NV? Oliver felt a huge knot in his stomach. First, the "greedy" guy he had to give the car to and now her. It was like someone was playing a very fucked up game of chess, and they were all pawns on his chessboard.

Oliver rose. The blood left his face as he stepped over the wet towel at his feet and stood next to Jessica, whispering to her ear.

"Meet me at the Kung Lei Chinese restaurant later tonight."

GLUTTONY

Matthew walked in circles around his living room. If only he could contact NV. Every time he had tried, it just led him to dead ends. Matt wasn't even in the mood to cook; he had been anxious all day, expecting an answer on what to do next. His only instruction had been to wait after sending the video of torturing the poor bastard in his basement. A few hours later, he had received another text. This one only informing him that someone would knock at his door. All Matthew had to do was let the man in and do whatever he wanted.

What if the man was a cop? Or what if someone was sent to kill him? No, impossible. NV had said that he still had plans for Matthew. However, he might as well be lying. Extortion and blackmail seemed to be right up the hacker's alley, so deceit could be added to the list. In any case, Matt had no choice but to do as he was told.

The doorbell rang. Matt stood petrified. Never in his life had he felt like the prey instead of the predator. It was a feeling he did not enjoy in the slightest.

Finally, he armed himself with enough courage to answer as the bell rang again, this time more sporadic as if whoever was on the other side was pressing the button frantically.

Matt didn't even bother to see through the peephole before opening the door. He assumed that he wouldn't recognize whoever was on the other side anyway.

And he was right. A tall, built man, whose bald spot stretched down until forming a crown of gray hair around the sides of his head, stood on his porch. The man's gaze was piercing, penetrating. Matt recognized those eyes. It was the look of anticipation from someone who was ready to inflict some serious pain.

Matt stepped aside. The man gave him a nod as he entered.

"Where is he?" The man asked.

"He's in the basement," Matt replied coldly.

Without skipping a beat, the man strode through the house, looking frantically for the entrance to the basement.

"It's in the kitchen," Matthew said as he followed.

The man went to the kitchen, found the door, and went downstairs. He didn't even bother to switch the light on. Matt flipped the switch as he stepped down.

In the middle of the large basement was Brian Thompson, who had spent the last couple of days tied to a chair, blindfolded, with dried sweat and blood covering his naked torso and his pants stained with piss. Brian woke up, startled at the sound of footsteps.

"P-Please," Brian whimpered. It was his favorite word. "Let me go. I won't tell a soul."

The old man knelt in front of Brian and ripped off the blindfold.

"You remember me?" the old man asked. "Do you know who I am?" Brian kept silent, his eyes shaking. "You son of a bitch. You don't even have the balls to remember the lives you've ruined. I'm Trevor Bates."

Brian's eyes widened, he started jerking his head side to side. "No! No! What're you doing here? Wha-what's going on?"

"Payback," said Trevor as he punched Brian in the nose.

Brian's head swung to the side with a cracking sound. A river of blood flew out of his nostrils and mouth.

"P-Please . . ." Brian begged, spitting red on the floor. "I'm sorry . . . I didn't mean what happened. I was drunk…"

"What's that?" Trevor shot back. "You're sorry? You're fucking sorry? You took everything from me!"

"I paid for my crime . . ."

"A couple of years on parole and community service doesn't feel like enough payment. You ruined my life. You fucking piece of shit. You got drunk and innocent people had to pay the price. If it wasn't for you, I would've woken up this morning with my wife in my arms. If it wasn't for you, my daughter would've been graduating high school by now. If it wasn't for you, I wouldn't have become the monster that I am now. So tell me one, just one simple fucking reason as to why I shouldn't cut your balls off and make you swallow them."

Brian was now hyperventilating, his eyes bloodshot, whimpering like a defenseless pup. "It-it was an accident . . ."

Matthew cringed. *Wrong answer, pal.*

Trevor stepped back. He turned to Matthew and looked him dead in the eye. "You got tools?"

Matthew nodded, a gleeful smile on his face. "Yessir."

"Bring them. I've heard you make one hell of a stew."

PRIDE

Timothy sat in his office with the cellphone pressed tightly against his ear. It had been a stressful morning. Somehow, he had managed to avoid two meetings and cancel a couple of appointments for that day. He had spent the rest of his day making calls. He knew there had to be someone who could give him Nicolai Vines' personal phone number.

Finally, he had gotten ahold of Vine's assistant, and while the guy had given Tim a hard time, it only took a bit of pressure and smooth talk to finally convince him to hand the phone to Mr. Vines himself.

"Nicolai Vines speaking," the man on the other line declared.

"Good morning, Vines. This is Timothy Wilson . . ."

"Oh, Timothy, what a pleasant surprise," Vines interrupted. His tone didn't sound pleased in the slightest. "My assistant says you're eager to talk to me about something. From the sounds of it, it seems important, so let's get straight to the point."

Tim had to bite his tongue to not shoot back a sarcastic remark. "Indeed, it's a business idea that I think you'll be interested in. However, I can't discuss it on the phone, so . . ."

"Why not?"

"I would prefer to talk it over with a cup of coffee."

Vines paused. "As a matter of fact, I have some time to kill right now."

"Right now?"

"Yes, right now. Unless it's not convenient for you . . ."

"No, no. It's perfect. Let's meet at Coprei's Café. You know where it is?"

"Of course. I'll meet you in ten minutes."

Vines hung up. Timothy stared at the phone, surprised at how easy it had been to convince him. If Vines was indeed the hacker, then he might've smelled something fishy going on. Still, it was a risk worth taking.

The café stood across the street from the office building. Nicolai had been quick to respond and even quicker to arrive. As soon as Tim sat down on one of the outside tables of the café, Nicolai gave Tim a pat on the shoulder. Had he been waiting for Tim? They shook hands as Vines took a seat. Vines was the first to talk.

"Sorry to say this, Tim, but I don't have much time on my hands, so let's not beat around the bush. You said you had a killer business idea?"

Tim settled in his seat, taken aback by the particular choice of words, and cleared his throat. "You see, Vines. I've heard that, besides all of the businesses you have scattered throughout the city, that you also indulge yourself in more . . . unconventional lines of work."

Vines raised an eyebrow. "What do you mean?"

Tim shrugged. "You know what I mean. The kind of business that brings you loads of cash really quickly. The kind people kill for."

"I'm sorry, Tim. I have loads of eggs in a variety of different baskets, so I'm not sure exactly what you mean."

Don't play dumb with me.

"I know what you do," Tim said sharply. No more playing around.

"Assuming that I'd know what you're talking about. Does that mean you want in on it?"

"It means I know who you are. And I won't play any of your games. I'm not your pawn."

Nicolai let out a chuckle. He leaned in on the table and whispered. "Life is a game, buddy, and everybody is a pawn to those who know how to play it."

Nicolai stood up, buttoned up his suit, and walked away from the café with a devilish smirk on his face as he crossed the street.

Timothy didn't bother following him. If Vines was indeed NV, then he would know that Tim was onto him. No more hide and seek.

Not a minute after Nicolai disappeared into the crowded streets, Tim's pocket vibrated. A message from NV.

Bold. Even for you, Pride. This is a dangerous game you're playing. Your next task is not going to be easy.

I won't be part of your next task. Timothy texted back. *This is over.*

Not if you want to survive. NV replied.

Tim tried sending another message threatening to call the police, but it came up undeliverable. Even if it meant sacrificing his career and the relationship with his wife and children, Tim couldn't allow this sham to continue. Who knew what kind of sick and twisted mission that psycho would send him on? Not to mention that he'd be participating in ruining other people's lives.

What if the police find out I dug up a body and brought it to the city? What if I'm blamed for their murder? I could be incriminated. I need to run away. I'll take my wife and kids with me. I'll disappear. Start over somewhere else.

It wasn't the best plan, but it was definitely better than a life sentence.

LUST

The Chinese restaurant Kung Lei was near the city center. Not in the main nor busiest avenue, but in one of the adjacent streets. One of those that are so narrow they seem like alleyways; the kind of corner where homeless people would seek refuge, placed near a dive bar and abandoned shops with boarded windows. However, despite the gloomy atmosphere surrounding the place and the fact that it had no place to park, profits rose every month. The type of business being carried out there had nothing to do with food.

It was hard to believe that someone with such a reputation as Nicolai Vines would hang out on that side of town. Jessica was sure that was the intended idea, to make it look as if he had set up a restaurant for the hell of it, just because he could, or just to have another stream of income, no matter how small.

Well, it had paid off, at least for Jessica, who, after seeing him in one of the clubs he owned, would never have thought that the impeccable businessman would come anywhere near such a place.

Jessica turned to Oliver. The boy had called for one of his close friends to keep an eye on his cousin Freddy for the rest of the night. She could see he wasn't entirely comfortable with the decision, and her heart ached for that, but desperate times demanded desperate measures.

Oliver and Jessica met at the place designated by Oliver. Jessica had the discretion to change clothes, putting on slacks and a hoodie that covered her almost completely. She had also put on some makeup in a different way than what she'd usually wear. Instead of covering small imperfections such as dark circles or expression marks, he stressed them. Jessica knew that, with the right touch, she could become almost unrecognizable. And she knew she had done a good job when Oliver walked by her side without even seeing her. She was the one to approach him.

"Wow, are you okay?" the boy asked. "You look like a crackwhore."

"I know, hun. That's the point," she looked around warily. "What exactly are we doing here?"

"You wanted to find Vines, right? This is where his crew hangs out," he said, signaling the restaurant.

The streetlamp flickered. Jessica felt the cold breeze embracing her. Maybe this was not such a good idea.

"What made you change your mind?" Jessica asked. "I mean, before, you just wanted me out of your house, yet you came here too. You could've just given me the address and have a clear conscience."

"I wouldn't. There's no way I'd have a clear conscience, especially if I know who you're dealing with."

"So you do know Vines. He's not just your supplier."

"Not really. I've never even met the guy. But that hacker you talked about, I know him. You're not the only one that son of a bitch has been harassing." Oliver pulled a joint out of his pocket. With a swift movement, he lit it up and inhaled. He held his breath for a bit before continuing. "If there's the smallest chance I can see him face to face, I want to be there. Besides, a woman all by herself in a place like this, you may need some protection."

Jessica looked him up and down. "I appreciate the thought. But don't get me wrong, you're not exactly a heavyweight. I could kick your ass easily."

Oliver rolled his eyes as he let the smoke out. "Thanks for the compliment."

"It's okay if you want to go back," said Jessica. It was sweet what he was trying to do, but he would probably do more harm than good. "I can figure out the rest on my own."

"Nope." Oliver stood in front of her. "I'm your contact. This is my turf. They'll be wary of a new face."

"You just told me you've never met the guy!" Jessica snapped. "I, on the other hand, have met him once. Besides, if he's our guy, then he knows who we both are anyway."

Oliver opened his mouth to reply, but he stopped, his jaw wide open as his face paled. Jessica felt the cold touch of metal even through her hoodie on her upper back. A voice from behind her made all the hairs of her body stand on end.

"Don't do anything stupid, and everything will be fine."

"L-Look, man," Oliver stuttered, raising his hands. "We're just here to talk to someone. I'm one of you. We just . . ."

"Shut the fuck up," the man ordered. "Go to the restaurant. And if you do anything funny. I'll put a bullet in her."

Oliver nodded and turned around, both hands still in the air. The man pushed Jessica forward, and she followed the boy to the restaurant. The place was immense and elegant on the inside, a stark contrast to the outside appearance. A pattern of red and gold colors on the chairs, walls, and ceiling, only illuminated by the light of the candles spread throughout.

In the middle, on one of the largest tables, a man on a tuxedo sat comfortably with a glass of red wine in his hand. Jessica could recognize the man from a mile away.

Nicolai Vines rose from his chair, his face beamed as he watched them walk toward him.

"Well, isn't this a surprise," Nicolai declared. "I wasn't expecting any visits tonight."

Oliver was the first to talk. "S-Sir, I think this is a misunderstanding . . ."

"A misunderstanding?" Nicolai put the vine glass down and rested his hands on the table. "No, this is exactly what I was expecting."

He snapped his fingers. The man who had been pointing a gun at Jessica and Oliver stood beside his boss. Jessica felt her lungs tightening. How did Nicolai know they were on to him?

"The last couple of days have been pretty exciting for the two of you, haven't they?"

They both kept silent. Nicolai sauntered around the table and stopped just a few feet away from them.

"Whatever you're doing," Jessica started. "You're not going to get away with it."

Nicolai jerked his head back, mock surprised at her boldness.

"Oh, sweet innocent girl. Of course, I am. *You*, on the other hand, not so much."

Someone's phone beeped. Nicolai turned to his bodyguard, his gaze stern.

"Really, Craig? Turn that shit off."

Craig nodded and pulled out his phone. Nicolai stared at Jessica and Oliver as he reached into his jacket. Jessica swallowed when she saw that he had taken out a gun and aimed it at them. "You got five minutes to explain yourselves," Nicolai ordered. "What are you doing snooping around my property?"

Behind the kingpin, his bodyguard's eyes widened while looking at the screen of his phone.

"Sir, Mr. Vines," Oliver started. "We weren't doing anything. I swear."

"Oh, yeah?" Nicolai waved his gun, a mocking smirk on his face. "Then, explain to me why Mr. Roca, one of my closest associates, warned me about a woman looking for me, one who looks coincidentally a lot like the one standing in front of me. In the same week that the leader of the Third Street Soles told me that a car full of weapons had been stolen from them by a guy whose physical description is also pretty similar to yours. Isn't it safe to assume that your two have been the ones fucking around with me?"

"Wait . . ." Jessica started. Nothing made any sense. Something was wrong, very wrong.

Craig's face paled.

"I don't want to wait anymore," Nicolai declared. "I've been waiting enough tonight. I sent a few of my teams to look for the two of you, and even so, I still figured that you'd come straight to me eventually."

Craig pulled his gun out of the holster.

"Look out!" Oliver yelled, but it was already too late.

Nicolai Vine's head jerked forward as a deafening bang spread across the room. His left eye flew out of its socket in a mixture of blood and smoke.

Jessica and Oliver jumped back in horror as Nicolai's body fell limp on the wooden floor. Nicolai's bodyguard stood there, his hand gripping tightly on the gun and shaking. He seemed to be as shocked as everyone else.

Jessica dropped to the floor and snatched Nicolai's 9mm. Craig lowered his weapon, put it back on the holster, and raised both hands.

"You two need to get out of here," he said.

"W-What?" Oliver asked, his eyes switching between Jessica and Craig.

Craig put his phone on the table. "Take it! NV is not done with you two."

Then Craig ran away in the opposite direction.

Jessica put the gun in her jacket while exchanging puzzled looks with Oliver. He seized Craig's phone from the table as he stepped over Nicolai's corpse.

"We have to get the fuck out of here."

SLOTH

The black and purplish night sky cloaked over two shadowy figures running between buildings, lost in a maze of concrete. Oliver and Jessica stopped in the middle of a suffocating alleyway. The walls of the buildings were so close to each other that it felt like they were going to squish them in.

Oliver closed his eyes and leaned against one of the walls, ignoring the claustrophobic feeling that threatened to overwhelm him. Beside him, Jessica struggled to catch her breath. She leaned forward, bent her knees, and puked on the ground. He looked elsewhere, disgusted but unable to blame her for it.

"What the fuck happened back there?" she asked, struggling to fight the gag reflex.

"It wasn't Vines . . ." Oliver gasped. "It wasn't him."

"Yeah, that's pretty clear," Jessica remarked. She straightened up and looked at the sky.

The phone. Oliver pulled it out of his jacket and turned it on. Thankfully, it wasn't locked by any passwords. He was on the home screen. If it was as bad as he suspected, then they were effectively fucked. He clicked on the messages app and found what he was looking for. He read it to Jessica out loud:

"Despair. I know your struggles. I know your fears. I know what you've been doing behind closed doors. Those pictures you've taken. Those videos you've recorded. Those lives you've ruined. It will all be exposed for the world to see unless you put a bullet in your boss's head. Give this phone to the man and the woman. If one or both of them dies, then I'm sure you'll be smart enough to infer the consequences. I still have plans for them. NV."

"What?" Jessica uttered. Her fingers went to her scalp. "This doesn't make any sense . . . Did the hacker just save our asses from Vines? How did he know we were there? And if he's not Vines, then who is it? What the fuck is going on?"

"J-Just relax, okay?"

"Relax?" Jessica yelled. "How am I supposed to fucking relax? We're at his mercy. There's no way to get out of this!"

Oliver looked back down at the screen. "Maybe we've been looking at this all wrong."

"What do you mean?"

"NV . . . Just reading it out loud makes me think that maybe it's not an acronym . . ."

Jessica tilted her head to the side. "What's your point?"

"The man you told me about, your friend, the one who's also been targeted by the hacker. What was his nickname? What did the hacker call him?"

Jessica shrugged. "I don't fucking know. It was like Arrogance or something like that. Pride, that's what the hacker calls him, Pride."

"The hacker calls me Sloth. What does he call you?"

Jessica jerked her head back, seemingly understanding where he was going. "Lust . . . why is this important?"

"Don't you see a pattern? Everyone who's deep to their knees in this shit is being labeled as one of the deadly sins. My mission was to meet a guy and give him some shit I stole. The hacker never told me his name, but when I asked the dude why he was doing this, he told me he was just greedy. Pride, Sloth, Lust, Greed . . . We're all pawns of this psycho."

"Yeah, but what about Despair? That's not one of the seven sins."

"I think it is. When I went to catholic school, we were told all about the deadly sins and shit, right? Well, my teacher told us that there used to be eight sins. One of them was called tristi . . . something, I don't know. It was in Latin, okay? It meant sorrow and despair. And there was another one that I don't remember the name of. But basically, some Pope back in the day combined those two sins into Envy."

"Okay, so this hacker is some sort of religious freak. What does that have to do with anything?"

"Think about it," Oliver stepped closer to her. "What if NV is not an acronym? It's N and V. N-V. En-Vy."

Jessica's patience seemed to be running short. "So, this hacker is Envy. That's what you're trying to say. How does that help us?"

Oliver took a deep breath. He couldn't believe she didn't understand what that implied.

"It's like you said. This hacker is probably someone who knows us, all of us. So think about it. Someone who knows us and envies us."

"Why would anyone envy us?" Jessica shot back. "I'm a prostitute; you're a junkie, maybe Tim, but still."

"Maybe we share something else in common. Something the hacker doesn't . . ."

Oliver let the words linger in the air. A subtle vibration in his hand startled him. Craig's phone lit up, popping a message on the screen.

"Lust and Sloth. The most unlikely of alliances. I never thought the two of you would hit it off. I know what you're scheming. As you can see, I know everything. I have one last mission for the two of you. Each on their own, though. And if you refuse, well, let's say the consequences are now a bit direr. After this, not only will you not hear from me ever again, but I'll make sure to solve whatever issues you have left unresolved. You'll receive instructions on your respective phones. Craig's phone is for either of you to keep; I don't care who."

Attached there were a few video files. Oliver swallowed and locked eyes with Jessica. She nodded. With trembling fingers, Oliver pressed the play button.

The grainy image blinked sporadically, making it hard to see what was going on. It was recorded vertically and whoever was holding the phone seemed to be in some sort of lobby. Too fancy to be from a regular building, but not fancy enough to be from a hotel. Jessica gasped and covered her mouth with one hand.

"That's my apartment building," she whimpered.

"Where is she?" yelled a man on the video at the top of his lungs.

The camera focused on a man standing in the lounge. In front of the elevator stood a woman with a broom.

"I'm sorry, sir. I can't tell you anything about the tenants of this building. So, please, I'm going to have to ask you to leave, or I'll call the police."

"Call whoever the fuck you want!" the man yelled. "I want to know where she is! I know she lives here!" The man pushed the woman to the side and slammed the elevator button. "Jessica!"

The video ended. Oliver turned to Jessica. Her face turned white as paper.

"I'm guessing that's not good news," Oliver said.

"Definitely not."

The phone sent him to the next video. Oliver paused before it played.

"I'm afraid of what I'm going to find."

Jessica snatched the phone out of his hand. "You should be afraid of what's going to happen if you don't."

She pressed the play button. The new video was in a house. One Oliver was very familiar with. It was his aunt's living room. Her chubby figure appeared on the screen, wearing her old overall. Oliver could almost smell the freshly made brownies from the oven. Aunt Ana looked directly at the camera.

"You must be tired, sweetheart. Let me give you a cup of tea so we can sit and have a chat, shall we?"

She then turned and went to the kitchen. The camera looked down. The silver blade of a butcher's knife entered the frame. The screen turned black.

"This is bad, this is very bad," Oliver dropped the phone. His hands went to his head.

The world around him started spinning, he tried to get some air, but his lungs wouldn't allow him. Jessica grabbed him by the shoulders.

"Hey, hey! Calm down, Oliver, c'mon!"

His knees gave up. Oliver fell on his butt and leaned against the wet, grimy walls of the alleyway. Jessica sat next to him.

"Oliver, c'mon. Snap out of it. We need to . . ."

A hellish beeping interrupted her. It was from their phones. Oliver tried to fight the impulse, his mind and heart racing, telling him not to look, but his hand had a mind on its own. He checked and found a message.

"Go to the amusement park near Rockwood avenue. If you want to save your auntie, then you will have to go clown hunting. A life for a life."

Clown hunting? What did that even mean? Did the hacker want him to kill somebody?

"No, no, no," Oliver broke down in tears. "I can't . . . I can't do it . . ."

"You're gonna have to," said Jessica. "If he wants you to kill someone, then you're going to need this."

She put the gun she had taken from Nicolai in Oliver's hand. It wasn't the first time Oliver held one, but it felt ten times heavier than any other. Jessica rose to her feet.

"This is the final trial."

PRIDE

Several hours prior, right after Timothy Wilson had met face-to-face with Nicolai Vines, the city had been busier than ever with rivers of people flooding the streets. Tim had to push people to the side on his way to the bank, something that he would never have done in any other situation. But this was different; his whole world was about to turn upside down, so he couldn't afford to waste time on courtesies.

Tim burst inside the bank. There was nobody in line. He strode to the main receptionist as he prepared mentally for the social gymnastics he was going to have to pull off. After all, he wasn't going to make a small request.

"I need to withdraw all the funds from my account," he said.

The receptionist eyed him up and down. She requested his ID and debit card. He complied, and she began tapping on the keyboard. She paused for a moment before asking.

"Sir, you have 2.2 million dollars on your checking account. Currently, we are not allowed to let you withdraw that amount until you've talked to the IRS and . . ."

"Bullshit," Tim intervened. "This isn't a dividend from a stock; this is my money. Money I've already declared. I know how banking works, so you're gonna have to try a bit harder than that."

The receptionist simply displayed a row of white teeth on a fake grin. "Let me talk to my manager real quick."

"Please do."

She went along and came back with a man twice her age and size.

"Morning, sir. I've been told you want to withdraw the entirety of your funds from your account."

"That's right." Timothy made an effort to smile.

"The thing is, we don't have that much cash in the vault at the moment. The banks . . ."

"I know how the economy works. I know that what I'm requesting is a bit unconventional, but it is not unheard of and certainly not illegal. So I would very much appreciate it if you let me withdraw as much money as I can from my account."

The manager told Timothy to wait a bit longer and take a seat. Nearly an hour passed, and he was starting to lose his patience when he was approached by the same man as before. The man led him to the vault. In the entrance, someone swept his body with a metal detector while a suited gentleman stood in front of him with a notepad in one hand and a badge on the other. The man showed a message on a plain white paper asking if Tim had been kidnapped or if he was acting on behalf of somebody else. The note said to either nod or jerk his head as a response. Tim rolled his eyes.

"No. I'm not being kidnapped. And I'm not wired either. So if you'd please stop with this charade, I'll be on my merry way."

"Sir," the manager said. "As we told you, we don't have that amount right now. You're talking about . . ."

"Two million two hundred thousand dollars in cash, I know. I'm more than happy to take what you can give me, and I'll be back by tomorrow morning for the rest. You have a federal agent here, so you're considering the possibility that I have been kidnapped, which means that you're also open to the possibility of paying some amount, right?" The men exchanged glances with each other. "Just give me my goddamn money."

Timothy Wilson walked out of the bank with a backpack and a couple of cases full of hundred dollar bills that accounted for 1.4 million dollars. He was promised that the rest would be there by tomorrow. Otherwise, Tim had threatened to tarnish the bank's reputation. Someone of Wilson's caliber speaking poorly of a bank would certainly have negative repercussions on their stocks. They wouldn't allow that, so Timothy was sure they would deliver on their promise.

That was if he survived another night.

WRATH

Trevor would have never guessed that cooked human flesh smelled so good. The entire house was impregnated with the fresh smell of a barbeque, only a bit different, sweeter somehow. A thin mist danced upward from the skillet. Matthew was definitely a talented man. What was once Brian Thompson's right bicep now looked ready to eat with some white rice, barbeque sauce, and a couple of cold beers.

The process to get there had been . . . satisfying.

For years, Trevor had yearned for the feeling of satisfaction after enacting his revenge. He had heard it all before, how people who had their revenge never got a kick out of it. How most of those who avenge and correct the evils of the world never got that feeling of satisfaction or fulfillment. If that were the case, then Trevor was an exception.

Trevor always feared that after killing the man who had ruined his life, he would feel just as empty, just as angry. And while that was true to some extent, it was as if he had taken a huge weight off his shoulders. Like he'd been walking around with a black cloud over his head. The cloud was still there, only not so grim now, with a beam of light shining through.

What would his wife and daughter think of him if they saw him like that? Happy and fulfilled after killing a man and now waiting to eat some of his flesh? Trevor shook those thoughts out of his head. Now knowing that the bastard was no longer a threat to the world, it was definitely easier to have peace of mind.

"You're the quiet type, I figure," said Matthew as he put a glass of red liquid on the table in front of Trevor.

"I hope that's not blood," said Trevor. "I'm not that open-minded, you know?"

Matthew smiled. "It's wine."

Trevor smelled it just in case. Better to be safe than sorry. He took a sip. It was the good shit, expensive.

"How did you find out you liked to eat human flesh?" Trevor asked. "If you don't mind me asking."

Matthew sat across Trevor. "I'm a nurse at the Saint-Mary hospital. I help take care of some of the patients. When you spend enough time in a hospital, you start seeing some . . . peculiar things." He shrugged. "I guess I always found it appealing, you know. When you go to the supermarket and look around the frozen meats, chicken, beef, duck, it all seems appetizing, you know? You feel your mouth water as you think how you're going to season it, what kind of spices you're going to use. The first time I saw a fresh open wound from a kid who had been in a car crash. That's when I realized that I wanted to try it. Curious to know the taste, the texture. I looked up online and found there were people who had this fetish of wanting to be mutilated and eaten. I got hooked."

Trevor stared at Matthew in complete silence for a few minutes. "You're one fucked up son of a bitch. You know that?"

Matthew shrugged again. "Yeah, I've made peace with that."

"So you work at Saint-Mary's, huh?" Trevor contemplated the empty plate in front of him. It was the same hospital his wife had been sent to after the accident. His daughter had died instantly, while his wife had survived in excruciating pain for hours in her hospital bed before finally passing. Trevor's only consolation until then had been that his sweet little princess hadn't suffered.

"Yessir, still to this day. Even if it keeps me busy, I always try to make room for my hobbies."

The doorbell rang.

"You expecting any visitors?" Trevor asked calmly.

Matthew let out a sonorous sigh. "No, it's probably just my nosy neighbor Regina. I'll take care of her real quick."

"Have you thought about making her into a soup?"

Matthew chuckled. "All the time. But it would bring a lot of unwarranted attention, so I'm not risking it. Besides, I don't think she'd taste good."

Trevor took another sip of the wine. He heard Matthew talking to the lady. She sounded cheery and was asking too many questions. *Oh, you have a date? That's sweet. What're you cooking today? Smells delicious as always.* Just gibberish. Trevor's phone beeped. He checked on the message. It was his friend, the man who had made his longest dream a reality.

"Wrath. I have one last favor to ask. It's going to sound weird, but I promise that, after this, you won't hear from me ever again. I need you to scare the hell out of somebody. I want you to go to the amusement park on Rockwood avenue. Just stay there and wait for around an hour wearing a clown costume."

It sounded simple enough. Trevor stood up and grabbed his things. Matthew walked in after hushing the lady away.

"Are you leaving already?" Matthew asked.

"I got a text from our mutual friend," Trevor said, putting on his jacket. "It'll be quick, so if you still want me around, just save me some leftovers."

Matthew nodded as he headed to open the door. "Okay, do what you gotta do."

Trevor stopped before stepping outside.

"Do you happen to have a clown costume?"

GREED

Your last trial . . .

That's what the hacker's cryptic message read. Roger sat beside his mother's bed in the hospital as he stared at his phone screen. As much as he reread the text, he still couldn't grasp what he was asked to do.

There was no way Roger would go that low. He was no saint by any means, but stealing was very different from what the text said. Murder? He couldn't, not even for the million dollars in cash that had been promised. There was a limit as to what he was willing to do. Stripping someone of their belongings on most occasions was nothing more than an inconvenience for the person, depending on how rich the person was, but even then, it's usually nothing worse than that, but taking someone's life was a whole different level entirely. It was the ultimate transgression. A sin without forgiveness. Something that ruined the lives of everyone around the deceased. Not to mention the fact that the victim will cease to exist. Everything they could've done, what they could've been, would be gone forever.

Roger clenched his hands on the arms of his chair, trying to hold back the tears. He had to refuse, but at the same time, he was afraid of the repercussions. This person had managed to not only hack him but several people, making them part of his sick game. For Roger, the money had been a good enough offer, but who knew how far that maniac would have gone to convince other people. And taking into account everything he had been told to do, he had no doubt that NV had ruined more than one poor soul's life.

Roger looked up at his mother, who laid peacefully on her bed. He detailed the outlines of her face. Despite the wrinkles decorating her skin and the gray hair resting ragged on the pillow, she was as beautiful as when he was a child. Back when she used to take him to the park on the weekends, buy him ice cream, and let him watch cartoons until bedtime.

Roger never had a lot of friends. But it didn't bother him much. He never needed the company of others to have a good time. After he graduated high school, he didn't hear back from anybody in his class ever again, and while he was not an outcast by any means, he enjoyed being on his own. He never actually missed anyone.

Most of his relationships would only last a few weeks, and those that lasted longer felt more relieving than painful once they were over. And he was fine with that. The only person he couldn't be apart from was his mother. Even a few days without visiting her felt like he was neglecting her.

Roger stood up, stroking the old woman's hair. He leaned over and kissed her forehead. He couldn't help noticing that the beeping of the machine was slower, each exhalation weaker and farther in between. He stared at the screen, and his heart sank when the next beep didn't come. Instead, there was a long and high-pitched sound. The line never rose back.

"Help!" Roger called. It was as if he'd been soaked with a bucket of cold water. He jumped and ran to the hallway screaming at the top of his lungs. "Please, help! Somebody, please!"

Three men rushed to the room. One of them grabbed his shoulder and tried to take him to the hallway. Roger pushed the doctor's hand aside.

"Please, sir," the doctor said. "Wait outside for just a second. We'll take care of this."

The doctor slammed the door shut, and Roger was left wondering about his mother's fate. His fingers clenched on his scalp, his face reddened as he almost tore his hair off.

Roger had no other choice but to sit down and wait for an eternity. He wasn't strong enough to see his mother die. He knew it was unrealistic to think that he would outlive his mother, but every time the thought invaded his mind, he always found a way to scruff it away.

With his heart in his throat, he saw the doctor and nurses stepping out of the room. Roger shot up from the chair.

"How's she doing, doctor?" Roger uttered, out of breath. "Is she okay?"

"For now," the doctor said. "I'm going to be completely honest with you, sir. She doesn't have much time. We're going to try our best to keep her alive as long as we can, but I can't make any promises."

"C'mon!" Roger snapped. "This is your fucking job! You have to keep her alive! There has to be something you can do!"

"I'm sorry," the doctor shrugged. "We'll do everything we can, but at the moment, there's not much we can do . . ."

"What about that experimental treatment you told me the other day?" Roger asked with a lump on his throat.

"It's not that easy. You see, we have to contact experts, specialists who are already working on the treatment, which is expensive and cumbersome. Not to mention that, as I said, it is experimental, so it may not work at all, especially in the state she's in."

"I'll do it," Roger whispered, nodding frantically. "I'll get the money, just gimme 24 hours. You better start calling those experts of yours."

With no more else to say, Roger ran out of the hospital, willing to do whatever he had to do to save his mother.

GLUTTONY

Despite being the first time he stepped on that place, Matthew felt at home. Shortly after Trevor left his house, he had received his message, and he was now standing at his destination.

Matt made sure to turn off the oven before heading out. His marvelous dinner would have to wait. NV had told him that there was one last assignment for him, one he would enjoy very much. Matt only had to look around him to see the truth in that statement.

He stood in the middle of a huge meat processing plant. It was deserted, yet, the equipment appeared to be in perfect condition, and, after taking a tour inside the refrigerator, he found that the place had to have been in use until recently, despite its poor appearance. Matt could only deduce that the plant was probably in the process of being shut down, it would explain why all the equipment was still functional, and the sign outside that read: "For Lease."

NV had told Matthew where to find the keys to enter. He had also been told that security cameras were disabled. After checking that everything was in place, Matt went to the control room like he had been instructed. He could only wonder what kind of surprise NV had prepared him, yet the truth was that he had mixed feelings about the whole situation.

On the one hand, the hacker had blackmailed him in the worst way possible by displaying the body of one of his victims in his backyard. But, on the other hand, Matt really hadn't done anything different than what he would have done on his own. He just had to kidnap some low-life nobody, let him live longer than usual for someone else to come to kill him, and then share it at a delicious feast with his new comrade. And now, the meat plant.

Even though he had considered becoming a butcher after discovering his new tastes, he knew that he wasn't likely to make as much money as a nurse. Even when having the capital to open a business, it's never guaranteed to work out. Matt was satisfied with his regular job and his double life. But he had been sent to a place he found fascinating and had been promised a "prize." So he had decided to comply and see where things went. All he had to do was put on the clothes he had been told and leave the front door open.

Upon arriving at the control room, he found something peculiar. There were several monitors on one side of the wall; they were all on, providing a live feed of the entire place. Matthew had been told the cameras were off. He couldn't risk it, so he texted the hacker, knowing that it would probably bounce back.

It didn't. The message went through, and he received a text right afterward.

Sorry for lying. I was afraid you wouldn't show up if I didn't tell you the cameras were disabled. Don't worry, though. It's a closed feed that only goes back to me. When you're done, all the evidence of you being there will be deleted. This is just for me to keep tabs on what's going on and also a form of entertainment.

Matthew took a deep breath; his eyes fell on the chair in front of the monitors. There was a black apron, a couple of gloves, and a pig mask. He couldn't help but smile at that little detail.

He took off his shirt, tossed it across the room, stripped down, and put on the apron, gloves, and pig mask. Just as he contemplated his new self in the reflection of the windows spanning in the control room, the front door of the plant opened. Matthew saw a beautiful young woman step into the darkness through the cameras. The door closed shut behind her, startling her. She looked around, biting her lower lip and trembling, anxious.

The game was about to begin.

LUST

The darkness of the seemingly abandoned plant was abrasive, suffocating even. Jessica heard the door slam shut behind her and knew, with complete certainty, that she had made a horrible mistake. She should've never listened to the hacker. She should have gone straight to the police. But still, how would she know if the influence of that mysterious man did not extend to the edge of the law? After all, only one text message was enough to kill one of the most influential criminals in the city.

She opened her mouth to call out for someone but knew that it was probably a bad idea. Her instructions had been to go and wait. Nothing more and nothing less. The only reason she felt remotely safe was that the hacker needed her alive somehow to complete his twisted game, but that didn't mean he would need her alive after the "last trial."

A mechanical sound coming from some dark corner out of her field of vision made her take a step back. Just when her eyes were getting used to the darkness, a blinding light enveloped her. An ominous buzz flooded the atmosphere, metallic clangs and bangs all over the place. She had to blink several times to be able to open her eyes fully. The machinery had turned on. Rows of metal hooks glided in their predetermined paths. From a translucent curtain stained with red, hordes of meat came out hanging from hooks. The smell of blood mixed with the rusty air made her gag. Rows of exposed meat from what were once farm animals now enveloped the entire place.

Despite all the macabre imagery, she had remained relatively calm, nervous but put together, until she heard something that gave her goosebumps: The roar of a chainsaw. She froze in place.

Rows of pigskin and beef danced around her, disorienting her while she tried to locate the source of the sound. It seemed to come from all sides at once. Jessica turned around and darted to the entrance. She tried to open it, but the knob wouldn't budge. She was trapped.

No, no, no, no. There has to be another exit.

Jessica ventured to her right, pushing a cold sack of flesh out of her way. Jessica slipped in a pool of blood, fell on the floor, and struggled to regain her balance. A reflection from the corner of her eye startled her.

She gazed up to one of the dead pigs; one of them had a meat cleaver embedded deep into its skin. She felt a glimmer of hope as she grabbed the handle and pulled the meat cleaver out. Blood squirted out of the pig's open wound. She now stood vigilant, looking around her to find a place to hide or run away.

No, there was no way she could hide. Whoever was in the plant with her wouldn't stop until they found her. She could hear the purring of the chainsaw approaching, lurking inside the parade of dead meat around her. Jessica couldn't take it anymore.

"C'mon, you fucking coward!" She screamed at the top of her lungs.

The purring of the chainsaw became more prominent; it was coming from her right. Jessica prepared, clenching the meat cleaver with both hands. A spectral figure appeared among the flayed pigs, with a black apron covered in blood, dark gloves grabbing the chainsaw, and his face covered by a pig mask. The pigman raised the chainsaw and swung it down. Jessica dodged the spinning blades by mere inches as her butt hit the floor. She crawled back in desperation, out of breath.

The pigman raised the chainsaw once more. Jessica took the opportunity and shoved the knife into the man's thigh. She heard a muffled croak from under the mask, the chainsaw swept down, and Jessica rolled to the side. This time, the blades grazed her arm, slicing through the skin with ease. Jessica jumped to her feet as she covered her wound and darted in the opposite direction.

Jessica ran, barely aware of the wound on her arm. She made her way through the sacks of meat surrounding her. The whole world was stained in a red mantle, reflecting the yellow and opaque light of the bulbs. The chainsaw growled incessantly behind her, just a few steps away.

Jessica found an iron door, pulled it with all her might, and rushed into the darkness.

A faint mist covered the ceiling and floor of the room. The sacks of meat hanging from the hooks were wrapped in plastic. The cool air was omnipresent and embracive. She was stuck in the refrigerator room. Jessica crouched down and cuddled up in a corner. Her skin felt stiff and cold, as if she were made out of metal. The door swung open, accompanied by the drilling sound of the spinning blades.

Jessica stayed in place, her back against the icy wall, crouched while trying to control her breathing. Her gaze drifted to the ground, and her heart skipped a beat.

There was a trail of blood leading to her position.

SLOTH

The only thing Oliver Grant could think about was his family. Despite growing up in a humble home, he had always felt like he had everything he could ever ask for. Even though his father had never been able to keep a job for longer than a few weeks, or his mother had struggled with alcoholism for years, he had always felt loved and taken care of because he knew, in hindsight, that they had tried their best.

Losing them was the greatest pain Oliver had ever felt in his short life. But at least he had a wonderful aunt who took him in when he had nowhere else to go. His cousin Vinny, with whom Oliver always argued or picked on, but deep down, admired how hard he worked every day to put bread on the table. And his cousin Freddy, the one Oliver had grown up and played with despite the age gap. He was the one Oliver played with until that fateful accident that left Freddy bound to a wheelchair for the rest of his life.

They were the only people Oliver had left. If he managed to get out of this alive, he would not take them for granted ever again. He would cherish every second with them and do everything in his power to help them. If he didn't survive, he would at least die satisfied, knowing that he tried his best to save them.

The weight of the gun on his waist felt somewhat comforting, but not even a tank would be enough to calm his nerves as he walked through the deserted amusement park.

Oliver had not seen any security guards. He had simply jumped a fence and found himself wandering in the dark. However, he did notice security cameras scattered throughout the site, and he was sure NV was watching him.

Oliver walked aimlessly, looking for some clue as to where to go. He had to find a clown; that was his only instruction.

The Ferris wheel shone brightly over him in a multi-colored spectacle. The park was huge; trying to find somebody there would not be an easy task.

He closed his eyes, trying to remember the layout of the place. He had hung out there a few times during the summer when he was a kid. The horror house, the Ferris wheel, the rollercoaster, and the house of mirrors were all engraved fondly in his memories. He could almost smell the cotton candy in the air. There used to be a spot where a clown would sell balloons; he'd never bought one, though, since he'd never been a fan of balloons or clowns, for that matter. The sole image of a clown reminded him of the TV series "IT," which he had partially seen as a kid.

Then it struck him. The clown had to be in the only place Oliver had never enjoyed going, the one his cousin Freddy would always ask auntie Ana to take him to. The carousel.

Oliver took the gun out and gripped it tightly with both hands, pointing at the ground. He crept toward the direction of the carousel, guided by the memory of his child self. The dead, abrasive silence was only interrupted by the sound of his own footsteps.

He turned a corner and what he saw made his stomach turn.

Besides the carousel stood a lonely figure, their back turned to Oliver. The overall red and white stripes he wore contrasted with the blue and yellow balloons in his hands, not to mention the green, messy afro covering his head.

The clown.

Oliver raised his weapon and inched closer to the figure, slowly. He could feel all of the weight of his body on his heels with every step, now making a conscious effort to be as silent as he could. Oliver's hands trembled, cold sweat wrapping his palms.

As he approached, he realized that the clown was moving, although slightly. It was not a statue or a doll. It was a person.

Oliver couldn't believe what was happening. He was really about to kill someone, to take a human life. He never thought himself capable of something so terrible and, even so, there he was walking toward his victim, about to shoot him in the back of the head. The only reassurance to his conscience was that the man would not feel any pain and that Oliver's family would be safe in the end.

Finally, Oliver stopped just a few feet away from the clown, with the muzzle of the gun mere inches away from the green wig. He just had to pull the trigger. That's all he had to do. Oliver felt hot tears slipping down his face. His finger hovered over the trigger, unable to move.

This was going to end soon, one way or another.

PRIDE

"Please, tell me what's going on," Linda begged on the verge of tears. "Why are you doing all of this?"

Tim ran from one side of the room to the other, grabbing as many clothes as he could without even looking and shoving them into the big open suitcase on the floor. He bent down, forcing as much as he could before closing it and moving to the next one. "I told you. There's no time to explain," he said absently as he continued on his task.

"What kind of trouble did you get yourself into?"

Timothy stopped and looked her dead in the eyes. "Big trouble. And if you love me and our children, then you'll help me pack everything so we can leave as soon as possible."

Linda stood silent for a second, arms crossed, as Tim urged her with his eyes to start packing. She went to her side of the closet and started grabbing some of her clothes.

"Do you want me to wake them up?" she asked.

"No, not yet. I don't want to scare them. Besides . . ."

The doorbell rang. The husband and wife froze on their spots as their eyes shot in the direction of the main door. It was well past midnight; nobody should be up there at this hour. Besides, how could they even get to their floor? They lived in a penthouse. The only way to get to their floor was with a key.

"Linda," Tim rose to his feet. "Take the kids. Hide. Whatever happens, no matter what you hear, do not come out."

Linda's face paled. "But, Tim—"

"Damn it, Linda. For the first time in your fucking life, listen to me. Do it for the children. Go away."

Linda nodded and went on her way. Timothy crept out of his room and grabbed the baseball bat he had lying against a wall, gripping the cold metal as he approached the door. The doorknob shook frantically. Even if they had the key to the elevator, they would still need to know the password of the keypad to enter.

Tim pressed his ear against the door. He could clearly hear the beeping of someone punching the keys on the pad. He swallowed dry. Did the intruder know the password? He wouldn't be surprised if the hacker also knew the password to his house. He should have been faster, but it was too late to lament. The confirmation beep on the other side made his blood turn cold.

The door started opening as Tim slammed his entire weight on the door. It wasn't enough. As the gap grew wider, Tim decided to risk it. He stepped back. The door slammed against the wall and bounced back. A figure dressed in black stood at the other side. He wore a ski mask, his green eyes frantic. The masked man raised his hand, and Tim swung the bat. The tip of the bat clashed with the man's hand, knocking over the intruder's pistol to the other side of the living room.

Timothy dove toward the gun, jumping over a coffee table. He felt his own shirt pulling him from the neck from behind. A hand snatched him and dragged him, dumping him to the side.

Tim fell back against the carpet. He stood back up, grabbed the coffee table with both hands, and slammed it against the intruder's back. The table exploded in a rain of glass. The man fell to his knees, grunting in pain, only a few inches away from the gun. Timothy jumped on top of the man, wrapping his arm against the intruder's neck.

The intruder impulsed himself forward and managed to scrape the handle of the gun with his fingertips. Tim pulled harder on his choke. The man's head lowered for a second and jerked back up, knocking the back of his head against Timothy's nose.

Timothy felt the intense pain burn on his face as a trickle of blood spurted out of his nostrils. His grip loosened, the man in the mask dragged himself forward and snatched the gun off the ground. Tim pulled him, and they both rolled to the side. The man had the gun in his hand now and was trying to point it at his back. Timothy gripped the man's arm, doing his best to move the weapon away from him or make the intruder drop it.

The gun fired. A yellow flash illuminated the living room for a fraction of a second as the blast pierced through their eardrums. The man pushed Timothy off of him and stood up, struggling to regain his balance.

A small shadowy figure materialized from the darkness behind them, small arms wrapped around the intruder's legs.

"No!" Timothy yelled,

Jamie, his little boy, tried to push off his father's attacker to no avail and now stood dangerously close to the gun's muzzle. Tim reacted without thinking as he dove forward to save his son.

GLUTTONY

The chainsaw purred in the darkness. Faint clouds of cold mist enveloped the lower half of his body. It was mesmerizing to feel so much power. He was back on the hunt for new prey, this time served on a silver platter for him to play with. The pleasure that Matthew usually got out of his killings was never sexual, not really. But this time, there was an aphrodisiac sense to the ambiance. Maybe he would have fun with the girl before killing her. She would then be his first victim to satiate all of his desires at once. First sex, then the thrill of the kill, and of course, the saliva-inducing, heavenly dinner he would make out of her.

His eyes quickly got used to the darkness surrounding him. His sense of smell had been compromised by the mask, depriving him of his most useful asset and replacing it with the concentrated scent of latex. The sounds around him were muffled, so he could only rely on his eyes and sense of direction to guide himself amongst the labyrinth of hanging livestock.

A current of air whistled at his side. Matthew turned, holding the chainsaw firmly. Just another pig.

The wound on his leg throbbed. He was walking with a limp, yet barely aware of the pain, determined to find his prey.

A faint reflection on the floor made him stop in his tracks. He knelt, putting the weight on his good leg as he inspected what seemed to be small drops of blood. He slid his finger on the cold surface and saw the red shine brightly on his black finger glove. There was a barely noticeable trail of drops continuing and then taking a left. She was close.

You're mine now.

Matthew followed the blood as he licked his lips. Finally, he turned the corner, ready to raise the chainsaw once again. But only a piece of fabric laid next to a small red puddle.

She was gone.

The girl had covered her wound with her own clothes and moved on. Far from disheartened, Matt grew eager. It was a game, one she knew how to play. NV did not disappoint.

A clang echoed from the other side of the room. She had managed to reach the door of the refrigeration room and close it behind her. With no time to lose, Matt charged toward the exit with the chainsaw held high. He pulled the string a couple of times as he ran, and the purring motor of the chainsaw woke to full force, screeching and roaring as he sliced the meat around him.

Matthew pushed the door open with little resistance on the other side. The girl fell back on her butt. The look of horror on her face as she realized she hadn't been fast enough to lock him in, nor strong enough to stop him, was a thing of beauty. The hopelessness in her eyes was mesmerizing.

Matthew took a second to savor the moment as she desperately dragged herself back. He took one step forward. The girl kicked high.

Her foot landed on his groin, making him stagger back. She shot up and ran to the right. It took Matthew a second to recompose, his legs had instinctively closed, and he was now struggling to stay balanced. The familiar pain growing up in his pelvis made him dizzy, but nothing he couldn't control. It wasn't the first time a victim had kicked him in the nuts, and he had gotten used to walking it off.

He caught a glimpse of the girl moving up the stairs on the east side of the facility, skipping three steps at the time. Matthew's hand went for the cold metal of the handrail to propel himself upward, each step brought hellfire between his legs, but it would all be worth it soon.

Once he reached the top of the stairs, his eyes scanned the steel bridge in front of him. It led to a cubicle similar to the control room, some kind of office. There was no way for her to escape from there. She had dug her own grave.

He went for it. The sound of his boots echoed throughout the entire facility. He kicked the door open and barged in with a wide grin underneath the mask. All the lights were off. It was an office that oversaw the entire facility through a large, wall-spanning window. Nothing but a desk, a couple of sofas in a corner, and a large TV. No other exits. She was trapped.

Matthew gently placed one foot in front of the other, moving through the room like a shark in the sea. The air was so thick he could cut through it with the trembling blades of the saw, which he clenched tightly.

Then, a buzzing coming from the desk made him turn. A faint, white light shone from under it.

Found you.

Seven Sins

WRATH

Trevor turned around, definitely not expecting to find the image that now stood in front of him. A scrawny kid no older than twenty-something, pointing a gun at him with his bony fingers and about to piss his pants. Trevor just had to take one good look at the boy to realize he was probably one of those wannabe gangstas who were all mouth and no trousers. The kid wasn't even holding the gun properly.

Trevor let out an exasperated sigh as he scratched this head. The clown's wig was itching like a motherfucker.

"Really?" Trevor asked out loud. "This is the final trial? The grand finale?"

The boy's eyes widened. Trevor saw the kid's Adam's apple go up and down in a heavy gulp.

"Look, man, I don't want to do this," the boy shrieked. "But I have to . . . I have to."

Trevor tilted his head, the jingle bells in his costume clanging.

"This isn't going to end the way you think it is, kiddo."

The kid gripped the gun with both hands now. Even then, it didn't stop him from shaking.

Trevor raised his hand, the red glove on it, reflecting the lights of the bulbs above them, and placed it on the gun. He gently pushed the muzzle of the weapon away from him as the boy bawled his eyes out. It was a pathetic sight. The boy lowered the gun, his face red and covered in tears.

Trevor leaned his head back and then jerked it forth in a swift movement. His forehead hit the boy's nose.

The kid recoiled as both of his hands went to his face. The gun fell, bouncing off the concrete ground. Trevor dived for the weapon. The raggedy boy took off, running like lightning.

Trevor stood in his power position, pointing the gun straight at the boy's head. A clean shot.

Trevor pulled the trigger.

GREED

Roger barely had time to react. When he realized that there was a brat grabbing him by the leg, he was propelled back by the weight of Timothy Wilson, the man Roger had been assigned to kill.

Roger's back slammed to the ground with Timothy on top of him. There was a scream in the dark. The gun went off again as they struggled. Roger could feel a warm liquid on him while listening to the grunts and gruffs of Timothy Wilson.

Roger pushed Wilson aside while the boy, standing over him, kicked his ribs. A woman manifested out of the blackness, wrapped the child around her arms, and carried him out of harm's way.

"Get out!" Wilson wailed, short of breath. "Take the kids!"

Roger took his chance to strike Wilson's cheek with his elbow. The man let out a grunt of pain as Roger rolled to the side. He tried to stand back, groping in the dark for the gun. The woman dragged the boy back while he kicked and screamed at the top of his lungs.

Roger found the cold metal between his fingers and jumped up. He saw shadows moving from one side to the other out of the corner of his eyes. Instinctively, his hands went straight to them and pulled the trigger. One, two, three shots followed the shadows as they ran across the room.

A hand appeared from underneath him and pushed his arms up. Wilson slammed his whole body onto Roger, pushing him back toward the wall, knocking over a painting.

Roger tried to kick his opponent in the ribs, but the strength with which Wilson was pinning him to the wall was extraordinary. The lengths a man would go to save his family.

I'm only here for you, buddy, Roger thought as he slammed his elbow onto Timothy's back.

Roger grabbed Timothy's head with one hand, digging his fingers into the man's scalp, and pulled as hard as he could. He managed to lift one leg off the ground, with his back against the wall serving as support. Roger lowered his attacker's head and rammed his knee against Wilson's stomach. Wilson recoiled in pain. Roger took the opportunity to get off his grip. He lowered the gun back down and fired.

Timothy's shoulder was pushed back, spurting blood from a hole formed in a fraction of a second. Roger backed down the wall until he was a few feet away from his victim. He raised the gun with both hands and aimed straight at Timothy's chest.

The city lights below illuminated the apartment in lugubrious blue highlights. Timothy Wilson was scraped, a red spot soaking his expensive shirt. His face was battered and bloodied. It was a horrible sight, that of a broken man.

"Tell him I don't care," the broken man said. "I don't give a fuck about myself anymore."

Roger stood in silence, his finger lingering over the trigger, hesitant. He didn't want to do it. This man had a family, people who would miss him. But what else could he do? If he didn't complete his task, then he would lose the only person who had ever cared about him.

"I'm sorry . . ." Roger whispered.

Timothy chuckled. "He's playing you, you know? What makes you think he's told you the truth? You're nothing but a puppet. The only reason why I'm at the other end of that gun is because I got tired of being a pawn."

"I-I don't have a choice."

"That's what I thought too until I realized that I don't give a damn about money or my reputation. Not anymore. The only thing I really care about is my family. Nothing else matters."

Roger took a deep breath. "Family. You're right. Nothing else matters."

Roger shot. The ear-splitting bang spread in the living room and was then accompanied by a sepulchral silence.

It was hard to tell if he had hit his target. Timothy stood on the spot for a second before lunging forward. Roger reacted quickly, raising his arm and smacking Timothy on the side of the head with the butt of the gun.

Timothy ignored the hit and grabbed Roger by the shoulders, pulling him back with him. They both clashed against the wall-spanning window. A huge crack manifested and webbed in all directions. Timothy stepped back and then slammed both of them again. The crack grew wider. Roger placed his foot on the glass to propel himself back and freed himself from Wilson's grasp. The crack covered the entire window now.

Roger raised his gun once again and stood in silence as he saw the city's landscape behind Timothy.

"Do it!" Timothy screamed. "What are you waiting for!"

Roger glanced briefly over his shoulder to see the woman dragging two kids toward the front door. Both kids were screaming at the top of their lungs, their high-pitched screech piercing his eardrums. They were yelling out for his dad.

Roger felt like he'd been punched in the gut. He was about to destroy a family and rip them apart. But he was doing it for a good reason, right? So he could keep the only family he had left, the only one he ever had. A life for a life.

"I love you," Timothy confessed to his children, his back leaning against the fragile glass.

"I wish it didn't have to be this way," Roger said as he closed his eyes.

He pulled the trigger, not once, not twice, but three times. Each shot slammed Wilson's body harder against the window. Finally, the glass shattered into a thousand pieces as Timothy Wilson's body fell into the void.

LUST

Jessica was crouched in a corner, leaning against the wall and making a monumental effort to stay quiet. Even so, her lungs demanded more air, as if she were suffocating. She could hear the roar of that damned machine, but she wasn't sure where it came from. The only thing she was sure of was that it was inching closer. She didn't know what was worse, the certainty that she would die, or the conflicting glimpse of hope growing inside her.

If she had known that the place she entered to take refuge in was a dead-end office, she would have gone to another place instead. However, there she was, trapped in a fetal position in the corner of the room, certain that she had dug her own grave. Unless . . .

Jessica felt her hoodie's pockets. There were two cell phones, hers and Craig's, Vines' bodyguard. Without wasting any more time, Jessica slipped away from her hiding place. Heavy footsteps stomping on metal approached at a fast pace. She put her phone on the floor and threw it forward, letting it slide under the desk.

She then returned to her hiding spot behind the sofa. She activated Craig's phone, squinting as the brightness of the screen blinded her momentarily. She lowered the brightness to the minimum and proceeded to call her own number. A thunderous sound startled her. She managed to cover her mouth with one hand as she brought the phone to her chest, covering the screen.

The roar of the chainsaw was now coming from inside the room. The pigman took slow, deliberate steps closer to her position. From under the desk, a white light appeared, accompanied by a vibration on the floor. The pigman turned toward the light and slowly walked over to the desk.

Jessica held her breath. She could almost feel the blades of the chainsaw cutting the air. She didn't dare to poke her head out, so she stayed still like a statue. However, from the corner of her eye, Jessica could see the silhouette of the psycho.

The pigman pulled the chainsaw cord a couple of times until the machine erupted alive, louder than ever. An unbearable rattling echoed in the small room. The guy raised the saw over his head and swung down with all his might. The wood of the desk gave way easily, spurting a mist of sawdust in the air.

He stopped midway through. The pigman realized that there was no one under the desk.

With her heart pumping on her ears, Jessica emerged from her corner and lashed out at the masked pig. She wrapped her arms around his neck from the back, her foot stomping on the psychopath's thigh, digging in the man's open wound. He let out a guttural growl only comparable to that of an animal.

The pigman contorted from side to side, trying to shake her off and break free from her grip, but he couldn't do it without letting go of the chainsaw. In the midst of the struggle, Jessica caught a glimpse of the man's ear. The pig mask he wore didn't cover the whole head, leaving part of his neck and both of his ears exposed.

Instinctively, Jessica's teeth went straight to the ear, biting the soft flesh like a rabid dog. The man let out another growl.

She tightened her jaw harder, her mouth soaking in blood as her teeth dug deep in his skin. The taste of blood and sweat was horrid, but there was nothing sweeter than hearing the moans of pain from that hellspawn.

She pulled so hard that her head jerked backward with a piece of ripped ear still in her mouth. The butcher's hands finally released the chainsaw and went straight to his face.

Jessica released him and dropped, hitting her back against the floor. She dove toward the chainsaw while the pigman shook frantically in pain, both hands covering the left side of his head.

She snatched the chainsaw from the floor and ran out of the office toward the metal platform. Jessica stopped and placed the chainsaw on the ground, trying to remember how to turn it on.

Her head was spinning. However, even with adrenaline pumping in her veins, the taste of blood in her mouth and the sweat sticking to her clothes, she found peace of mind to grab the chainsaw handle as she had seen other people do. She then pulled the cord. Nothing. The pigman stood at the office's door; he looked bigger than ever before and started sprinting to her.

She pulled the cord again. The man was now just a few feet away, his hands reaching out to her, straight to her throat. Jessica pulled one last time.

The chainsaw roared with the ferocity of a lion. The vibration was so strong that it trembled her entire body. She lifted the chainsaw with all the strength that her exhausted arms could gather, letting out a desperate scream.

The blades cut through the pigman's groin. A cloud of blood spurted out from between the man's legs as he shrieked in pain. Instead of stopping, she lifted harder until the saw was now to the height of his belly button.

The agonizing screams of the man spread throughout the facility. In an outburst of anger, Jessica released the machine.

The chainsaw crashed to the ground with the blades still spinning while the bowels of the pigman rained on the floor.

He stood there for a second, a mix of shock and anger reflected in his eyes as he tried to keep his own intestines from falling out before dropping to the side with a clang.

Jessica let out a deep sigh while the man writhed in a pool of his own blood and entrails.

She let her body fall back in exhaustion on the cold, metallic floor of the bridge. She brought her feet toward her body in a fetal position and started sobbing. They were not tears of sadness or joy but tears of tremendous relief.

She stayed there and wept until her eyes had dried out.

Jessica slowly stood up, trying to avoid looking at the corpse in front of her, but her eyes seemed to have a mind of their own. She stared for a while at Mr. Pig's lifeless body, deciding whether it was worth it to try what she was thinking or not.

The rusty smell that impregnated the place, combined with the aroma of fresh blood, made her dizzy.

Jessica decided to give it a try. Anything that could get her some sort of clue of her captor's identity would be worth it. Because that's what he was, a captor. NV may not have her physically captive, but her mind and very soul were his to do his bidding, and she wasn't going to take it any longer.

Jessica leaned over the body, gathering all of her willpower to not vomit. Finally, she gathered enough courage to grope the corpse's clothing. Nothing. She stood back up and turned around. Did that man not have any car keys? No wallet? No cash? How would he even end up there? And how would he communicate his mission as accomplished without a phone? Granted, NV was likely watching the events unfold from the security cameras anyway, but still, he would need a way to communicate to his pig puppet somehow.

There was no reason to think that the main threat had been taken care of. Someone could still be lurking around in case things didn't go as planned, but she doubted it.

Even someone like NV probably would not see it coming that a 5'1" woman could take on a 6'2" bloodthirsty psycho with a chainsaw.

Jessica limped her way through the facility, checking every inch of the place for some sign of the killer's identity. All exits were locked, so it wasn't like she had any choice but to look for keys anyway.

After a while, she found the control room. A set of computer monitors hung from a wall, all of them on and displaying every corner of the facility. On one of the chairs lay a set of neatly folded clothes. Jessica snatched them from the chair and started examining them. A cell phone, keys, and a wallet. Exactly what she had been searching for.

She turned the phone on. The home screen was locked, so she wouldn't be able to use it without the password or a fingerprint. She cursed out loud and opened the wallet to find a couple of twenties and a bunch of cards. She was dumbfounded to find that pigman was not only decent-looking but somewhat attractive. His bald head and scruffy beard hid a babyface and blue eyes that seemed unable to hurt a fly. She had never found a better example of deceiving looks.

Matthew Walker. Next to his ID was another form of identification, this one from the Saint-Mary hospital. He was a nurse.

What a gentle soul, she thought bitterly.

It wasn't much of a clue, but this man was the only thing she had to go on. Far from discouraging, she felt compelled to find out who was responsible for all of her misery and put an end to it once and for all.

SLOTH

Oliver ran as fast as his legs allowed, the soles of his shoes barely touching the ground. He heard a metallic click behind him, faint but discernible among the stillness of the night. After that, a scream of exasperation and fury rumbled in the night.

"You fucking idiot!" The clown yelled. "You didn't remove the fucking safety lock!"

Oliver threw himself to the left. Successive shots thundered behind him. Dirt flew upward as the bullets whooshed past him, and he dove into the house of mirrors.

In the middle of the darkness, Oliver collided with one of the mirrors, his own reflection returning a look of terror and confusion.

He kept on moving, sliding his hand on the wall so as not to bump into another mirror. From the corner of his eye, he could discern figures moving around him. The fact he wasn't able to distinguish his own reflection from the shadows made him question his every step. It was like being surrounded by dozens of people circling around him like vultures waiting for him to die.

The ghosts in the mirrors moved erratically, without any direction. More gunshots cracked the air and glass alike. He could see flashes of light coming from all directions. Oliver ducked and hurried along with his head low. There were three or four clowns at any given time in his peripheral vision, with a twisted grin on their colored faces. A mirror in front of him exploded into a thousand pieces. Then another one at his side. Oliver stared at the ground, the world circling around him and his clothes clinging to his skin from the cold sweat.

There were diagonal lines of colors that interlaced with each other, reflecting in the mirrors and giving the illusion that the place was larger than it actually was. Oliver threw himself to the ground and began crawling, groping the lines on the floor to find the mirrors.

The shots became increasingly louder. Hot tears ran down Oliver's face as he crawled, knowing that he wouldn't be able to find a way out in time. He had imagined dying before, on his bed with a bong on his side and enjoying the best trip ever. But it never occurred to him that he would leave the world this way instead, being chased down like a dog, begging for his life in a dark, desolated corner of the world, and by the hands of the creepiest motherfucking clown he had ever seen.

Everything would be easier if he were high. He probably wouldn't be as scared, and maybe he would even embrace his fate. But instead, he found himself doing everything he could to survive. It was then that an image popped into his head, like a sign from God. It was crazy, but if it worked, it'd be poetic to think that his love for pot was going to end up saving his life.

He shot up from the ground and pulled his lighter out of his pocket, hoping that he would be tall enough. He lit up his joint and started wailing around the small flame above his head, as high as he could. He took a deep puff and then exhaled upward. He was now waving both hands, one holding the lit joint and the other with the lighter. He kept inhaling as much as he could and then exhaling it up to the ceiling. He could already feel his chest burning, the itching in his throat threatening to make him cough.

"I see yoooou!" sang the clown in a raspy voice, followed by a burst of maniacal laughter.

Another shot, the horrible noise tore up the air. The mirror at his side cracked and fell apart, his reflection disappearing from view.

Then, the fire alarm blared off, an angelic sound that filled him with hope. The sprinklers in the ceiling burst in a gleeful shower. On the walls, a red "Exit" sign manifested, arrows pointing the exact direction that he had to take.

Oliver rushed toward the red arrows, following them and feeling his salvation imminent. He started coughing on his way out, unable to hold off any longer, and his lungs strained due to the extra effort.

His body slammed against the metal door, swinging it open. Oliver inhaled the fresh, cold breeze of the night. All the colors around him started to jump out in stark contrast with the black sky. The lights became brighter. Red, green, and golden hues lit up, making him dizzy.

Oliver ran toward the rollercoaster, the only place he figured he could lose that maniac. He did not know how. He was guided only by the desperate instinct to stay alive.

Oliver ran past the carousel. The horses on it seemed to go faster than before, as if they were about to lose control and gallop their way out of the attraction. How did he even get into this mess? Nothing made any sense.

He climbed the steps toward the rollercoaster. The train stood in place, inert. Oliver looked up and saw a small platform at the side of the rails, high up on the last drop. He turned over his shoulder to see the killer clown sprinting toward him, gun held high, a devilish grin from ear to ear. Oliver glanced around, trying to find the control pad. He jumped over the waist-high, subway-like doors, stumbling his way to the train. To his right was the control panel. He ran toward it and started mashing buttons at random.

The safety bars came down from the seats, locking in place. A set of numbers appeared on a small screen on the side of the platform, counting down thirty seconds. The clown was now climbing the stairs to the attraction.

Oliver jumped on the train, trying to take refuge in between the seats. If that thing started off, he would have to find a way to hold on. The clown took two more shots, but they sounded different somehow, muffled. The clown was running out of bullets.

Facedown under the train seats, Oliver could see the giant shoes of the clown. He glanced over his shoulder and saw that the counter had only ten seconds left. He had to trick him somehow to get on the train, but he had no idea how.

The clown's heavy steps resonated on the platform as he approached. Oliver's cheek was pressed against the floor, and he wished he could disappear. The clown stopped. Oliver's heart skipped a beat.

Oliver jumped out of his hiding spot, hoping the clown was close enough to the train. The clown jerked his head back and raised his gun. With a swift movement, Oliver knocked the gun from the clown's hand. The 9mm bounced off the floor of the platform and toward the rails, disappearing between them in the darkness below.

The clown's face contorted into a grimace filled with rage. His hands went straight for Oliver's neck. His thick and stone-like fingers pressed on Oliver's jugular. Oliver carved his fingers on the clown's hands in a futile attempt to save his own life.

The train started to move. Oliver raised his foot and slammed it into the clown's ankle. The clown growled in pain as his grip loosened. Oliver shoved the clown to the side with the intention of making him fall on the train, but by the time he pushed the clown, the train had already left the station.

The clown fell on the rails. Oliver could have run in the opposite direction. He could've left and hoped that the clown wouldn't catch up to him. But in that split second, Oliver realized that wasn't an option. The clown would catch him sooner or later, or NV, for that matter. He was tired of running away from his problems. It was time to fight them head-on.

Oliver crouched and jumped onto the rails. He looked up at the last drop of the roller coaster and headed there. It was a steep climb. Oliver had to get on all fours to ascend. The clown shot up behind him and began his hunt. Oliver hurried up, glimpsing from the corner of his eye the train circling the roller coaster. In a matter of minutes, the train would reach them head on.

Oliver focused his gaze on the platform at the top of the railing as he climbed. Carnival music blared in the night at full volume, accompanied by the grunts and curses of the murderous clown just a few feet behind him.

The rollercoaster sped up as it turned upside down on one of the curves.

Oliver could feel the wood underneath his feet shaking.

The clown grabbed his foot. Oliver jerked to the side and started kicking. The clown's grip was strong, but he managed to land a kick square in the clown's red nose. A squeaky sound came with the cracking of his nose breaking.

"You son of a bitch!" the clown yelled.

The wood and metal underneath them trembled viciously. Oliver saw that the train was fast approaching. All of Oliver's muscles screamed in unison as he propelled himself upward. He reached the top of the rail and saw with horror the front of the train growing wider and wider toward them, full speed.

Oliver rolled to the platform at the side and closed his eyes.

The wind whooshed behind his back. The entire platform was shaking so violently, Oliver thought it would crumble. He glanced over his shoulder just in time to see the train slamming straight into the clown's face. The green wig flew in the air with a red splatter and a hollow thump. The train kept on its way, only slowing down as it approached the entrance of the rollercoaster and obediently stopping where it was supposed to, then lifting the security bars, ready for the next ride. The front car was covered in blood.

Oliver lowered his gaze and met a mangled body wrapped between the bars and wood underneath the rails. The clown suit was in pieces, along with bits of flesh and gore. The clown's head was contorted back in an impossible way, resting on one of the metal bars with an expression of dread and wide-open eyes gazing up. The left side of the clown's face was soaked in blood. The right side had the makeup still intact.

Oliver slowly stood up; his jaw hung open. He wanted to scream, but his throat had tightened, he wanted to cry, but his tears had run dry.

Slowly, he made his way back to the entrance of the attraction.

As he stepped down the wooden steps, something vibrated in his pocket. Oliver didn't even bother looking at the screen before answering.

"I did it," he muttered. "What else do you want from me, you sick fuck?"

A woman's voice came from the speaker. "Oliver? Oh, my God, yes! Thank God you're still alive!"

"Jessica?"

"Meet me at Saint-Mary Hospital."

"What? Wait, are you okay? What's. . ."

"I'm fine," she said sharply. "I-I need you to do something for me."

"What's that?"

"Do you know how to unlock someone's phone without the password?"

Oliver struggled to utter words out of his trembling lips. "I, uh, I picked up a few things from my cousin . . . but I'm not sure. Why?"

"There's no time to explain. I'll go get Timothy and then head straight to the hospital. Wait for me there."

He agreed, and she hung up. Oliver stared blankly at the screen, his brain still processing what had just transpired.

Once he reached the end of the stairs and out to the amusement park once again, he went to the bottom of the rollercoaster's structure. The foundation stood strong and shrouded in darkness. He used his phone's flashlight feature to illuminate his path.

Hidden between rubble and grass, the gun that had fallen now rested between the rocks under the rollercoaster. Oliver reached down and grabbed the handgun.

He contemplated the gun. It felt lighter than before. He took out the magazine and checked on the witness holes. There were only three bullets left.

Oliver put the magazine back and the gun on his waist. The only question left was how to get to the hospital. He had taken a taxi to the amusement park, half convinced that he wasn't going to get out of there alive, so he didn't even bother to think about how to get back. He didn't have a single penny on him, and the hospital was miles away.

He walked over to the fence that separated the park from the parking lot and climbed it. There was only one car. He didn't need to be a genius to deduce that it belonged to the killer clown. Oliver strode to the car, took off his shirt, and wrapped it around his arm. Closing his eyes, he smashed the window on the driver's seat and unlocked the door. The alarm blared in the silent night. He wasn't worried in the slightest. If nobody had come to his rescue after several gunshots, he doubted that anyone would happen to hear a fucking car alarm.

He sat inside as he maneuvered the cables under the board. He did as he knew, and the car's engine roared to life. Oliver smiled and put both hands on the steering wheel as he took a deep breath. His eyes wandered around the car. On the side-view mirror hung a picture. It was a man with his arms around a woman's and a little girl's shoulders. Despite the bright smile and cheerful demeanor of the man, Oliver recognized his eyes. They were the eyes of the clown.

Oliver bit his lip and tried to hold back the tears but couldn't resist the urge to let out a sob. It was as if a dagger had pierced his chest. He had taken that man's life. Even if the man had tried to kill Oliver, it still felt horrible.

Oliver cried all the way to the hospital.

ENVY

The room was shrouded in obscurity, the only source of light coming from the monitor on the desk. The silence was interrupted by typing on the keyboard. The screen presented all the information about one of the latest subjects.

The folder named Despair opened. Inside, it contained all the information of Craig Sunderland, the former bodyguard of Nicolai Vines. The one who had been visiting various compromising sites on the deep web over the last year, along with his home address, cell phone number, social security number, bank accounts, and all sorts of other intimate details.

Envy proceeded to delete all of it. Despair had fulfilled his purpose. If it weren't for him, Lust and Sloth would have had a shorter lifespan than expected. That could not be tolerated. They had a part to play in the game.

It was incredible how much one could earn on the black market for a couple of snuff films. These paid videos in which the "star" is killed or commits suicide were a booming sensation on the deep web.

And with so much power at their fingertips, it'd be foolish not to record the game results for later profit. Envy had spent a lot of time dedicated to the deep web, coding, decrypting, learning. And now, Envy was close to finishing the game, their very own magnum opus.

Bony fingers danced between the keyboard and the mouse. The cursor slid through the screen and switched cameras on the monitor. Lust had overcome her challenge. This was an interesting turn of events. It was almost certain that she would meet her demise at the meat processing plant. Yet despite all odds, she had not only come out alive but had also put on a big show for the cameras.

Gluttony lay on one of the bridges connecting the offices; his insides splattered all over the metallic floor, and blood oozing to the ground below. Lust moved from one monitor to the next, looking for something, a way out probably.

The chair creaked while Envy leaned back on it and considered the options. Chances were that she would still try to be snooping as she had been doing for the last couple of days. All it took was one mistake for Envy's identity to be uncovered, in which case, plan B would have to come into motion. It would be easy enough to get rid of Lust now that she had fulfilled her role.

With just the pressing of a few buttons, the cameras switched once again, this time displaying the amusement park. The last time Sloth was on display, he had been running for his life after Wrath had snatched the gun out of his hands. Such a pitiful way to die. However, the footage told another story entirely, one that was both bizarre and unexpected.

After seeing the footage, Envy expected Sloth to be lying on the ground with a hole in the middle of his head. Or, on the flip side, with Wrath being the one with his brain splattered all over the carousel. Instead, a camera high up on the rollercoaster captured the moment in which the train ran full speed toward both of them. They were climbing up, but Sloth had managed to roll to the side to the safety of a platform just before getting hit by the train. The train ran over Wrath, and his body flew, slamming over the chairs of the train as his wig blew into the night sky.

Wrath's corpse fell to the main support structure, mangling and twisting between the beams and steel pipes until it stopped midway through, hanging in a contorted manner.

While impressive, this unexpected outcome presented yet another challenge. Sloth walked through the wooden rails and stepped down the rollercoaster. He looked pale, the features of his face rough as if he had aged ten years. Sloth glanced at his phone. Immediately, Envy's hand clenched the mouse. A few clicks later, and the voice of Lust came bursting through the speakers.

"Do you know how to unlock a phone without the password?"

Why would she want to know that?

"I, uh, I picked up a few things from my cousin," Sloth muttered. "But I'm not sure. Why?"

"There's no time to explain. I'll go get Timothy and then head straight to the hospital. Wait for me there."

The hospital. She was talking about Saint-Mary hospital; there was no doubt about it. And they were going to find out the truth if they weren't stopped. Luckily, somebody else could still deal with both of them, and they were the only loose ties left.

Without wasting any more time, the hacker contacted the only person capable of stopping them.

LUST

Jessica only had fifteen percent of battery left on her cellphone. She was surprised to have been able to make the last two calls, the first one to Oliver to make sure he was alright and tell him where to meet, and after spending a good ten minutes trying to reach Timothy to no avail, the second went for the cab to take her to Tim's place.

She clamped in her hand the money she had ripped off the pigman's wallet, her foot tapping impatiently at the concrete. She turned off her phone and crossed her arms. It was a warm night, yet her skin was cold and stiff like ice. It had been like that even well after getting out of that horrendous place.

Two beams of light manifested in the darkness, blinding her. She squinted and walked forward with her hand up. The yellow car parked to the side as she strode close. The dark-haired man with a greasy beard behind the wheel eyed her up before signaling her to get in the back.

Don't look good enough tonight to call for shotgun, I guess.

Jessica sat inside the cap and told the address to the driver.

"Feeling alright, sweetheart?" the driver asked.

She glanced at herself in the rearview mirror; she looked like a dead person walking.

"Not really. Hopefully, I'll get better soon, though."

The man nodded. He didn't seem like the chatty type, and she was grateful for that. Her head rested on the window as she watched the streetlamps slide past. It was a gloomy night, with a purple hue reflecting on the clouds above.

Timothy had always been upfront with her about everything, his career, his marriage, his preferences. And if there was one thing Tim cared about the most, it was discretion, for obvious reasons. To the point where his behavior often bordered on paranoia. Yet, resourceful as she was, Jessica had had no problem finding out a bit more about him than he ever intended.

She did that with every client. It was a trump card in case things got ugly. They usually never got too bad, but she had trust issues, cemented by her ex long ago.

In Tim's case, she had figured out pretty quickly where he lived. After all, he was a public figure, and despite his efforts to keep his private life away from the public's eye, no one could slip past Jessica.

She had seen Timothy's wife and children only once, though. On the local news, during the live broadcast of the charity event that he'd held for Saint-Mary Hospital. But they've never met Jessica, so if the worst came to be, Tim's wife wouldn't be able to recognize her. In her current state, she doubted that even Tim would be able to recognize her.

Traffic started filling the busy streets. They were downtown, so despite the late hours, the roads were never completely empty. Still, finding herself in a traffic jam well past midnight was not exactly common.

"You can leave me here. It's only a couple blocks away." She proceeded to hand the money to the driver and left the car.

"Thanks, love," he said as she closed the door and crossed to the sidewalk.

She strode through the street, bracing herself. Not too far, blue and red lights flickered, a couple of squad cars parked to the side of a building, along with an ambulance. Yellow tape surrounded the entrance of the building. Jessica felt her legs grow numb as the realization hit her. It was the building Timothy lived in.

Jessica ran, stumbling her way through the crowd that had gathered around the edges of the tape. She had to push some people to finally get to it. She crouched under the tape and marched to the scene. A police officer turned over his shoulder and raised his hand at her.

"I'm sorry, ma'am, I need you to step away," he commanded in a polite tone.

"I live here," she lied. "I need to know . . ."

Before she could finish her sentence, her eyes locked on a woman sitting on the steps leading to the entrance of the building, a blanket over her and her two children. It was Linda. Jessica ignored the officer's attempts to stop her and strode to the woman who was bawling her eyes out.

"Linda? What happened? Where's Timothy?"

The woman looked up; her expression changed for a split second from grief and sorrow to confusion as she tried to identify Jessica.

"I'm . . . Mr. Wilson's assistant. He wasn't answering his phone, so I figured something was wrong."

The weeping woman seemed to be satisfied with that explanation. "He . . . he tried to stop him, but . . ." Linda shut her eyes and pierced her lips as if that could contain the pain. "He couldn't . . ."

Jessica turned her head to where Linda's gaze was fixed. Her jaw dropped in disbelief as she saw the gruesome scene. A car was parked in between the police cars and the ambulance. Its roof crushed in with a red splatter all over. The windows had been pulverized. A couple of medics carried a stretcher with a body on it. They zipped the bag close just in time for Jessica to see Timothy's expressionless face gazing up at the sky.

Jessica's hands went to her mouth and then to her heart as she felt a stabbing pain in her chest. Her eyes watered as a wave of grief and rage filled her veins. She felt as if her legs numbed, and she decided to sit down next to the newly widowed woman.

Linda's cries were deeper and louder than those of her children, who were probably still processing what had just occurred. That sound, along with the people chattering, cars passing, and a myriad of other noises, grew quiet until the only thing Jessica could hear was a buzzing.

After all the struggle and hardships, she was still alive, but it was now dawning on her that not everyone had been so lucky. Jessica hadn't been the only pawn in the hacker's twisted game. But she wasn't a pawn anymore. She was tired of doing someone else's dirty work; it had been one of the many reasons she had escaped from her ex's grasp, and if she had to face the horrors of her past to be free once and for all, then so be it.

With a deep breath, she rose, a look of determination painted across her face. Jessica headed to the hospital.

GREED

Roger rushed through the sterile walls of the hospital's hallway. Still drenched in his own sweat and the smell of blood tainted in his clothes, he cut corners and pushed aside nurses, doctors, and patients alike until he reached his destination. The bag he carried felt heavy on his shoulder.

Once he had finished his deed, he had received a message revealing the most likely place where "Pride" would have hidden the money. Lo and behold, it was right where NV had said it would be. However, the most difficult part had been to walk past Wilson's wife and children to get to the prize.

The woman had been hysterical, cursing, and screaming at the top of her lungs, demanding him to leave them alone. Roger wasn't going to hurt them anyway. He didn't even want to hurt Wilson. He only wanted the bag. And once he had snatched it off the floor, he went straight to the hospital, back with his mom.

His heart was still beating fast, filled with a mix of emotions that threatened to make him vomit. On one side, there was excitement, for he finally had what he needed to save his mother. On the other was a gut-wrenching wave of guilt and regret. He knew that he would probably go to jail for what he had done. Besides the fact that he had been masked, he didn't take any of the precautions he usually took when robbing, and he was sure that, sooner or later, his recklessness would come back to bite him in the ass. But he didn't care, not in the slightest. First, he would make sure that all of his mother's medical bills would be paid for and to put everything in motion for her to have the experimental treatment the doctor had told him about.

Now standing in front of his mother's room, Roger's hands shook uncontrollably. He swiped the sweaty palms on his pants and turned the knob. He opened the door, and his jaw dropped.

The room was empty. Save for a chair and a neatly folded bed, there was nothing in it. No one.

Roger stepped back. His head turned to the sides as his eyes frantically scanned the place. A nurse with a clipboard exited another patient's room. He hurried to her, getting to her in just two long strides. He grabbed her by the shoulder, the nurse jerked in surprise, almost dropping the clipboard.

"Where is she?" Roger barked.

"Wh-who?" the nurse mumbled.

"My mother! She was staying in that room!" He pointed at the door he had come from. "Where did you take her?"

The woman's face turned into a grimace. "She was taken to the emergency room. We tried to contact you, but . . ."

"Fuck!" Roger exclaimed. He could feel the blood rising to his face.

"Sir, you're hurting me," the nurse whined.

Roger released his grasp. Red marks from his fingers manifested in the woman's tender skin.

"Where's the emergency room?" Roger demanded.

She stroked her arm as he shot him a cold glance. "Ground floor."

Once again, Roger was at the mercy of his legs, guiding him to the stairs instead of the elevator. Time was running out. He made his way down, skipping several steps at the time.

He slammed the door open and rushed to the emergency room. In the hallway, however, he found the face he'd been looking for: Doctor Lewis, the one who had been attending his mother.

"Doctor!" Roger called out.

Dr. Lewis turned to face him. The look on his face, though trying to stay professional, seemed grim.

"Mr. Johnson, we've been trying to reach you all night."

"What happened?" Roger demanded. "Is she okay?"

The doctor sighed. "I'm afraid not. I regret to inform you that she has passed. Her heart gave out. We tried to revive her, but it was too late."

Roger's legs felt rubbery as if all of a sudden they had turned to liquid. This could not be happening after all of his trials. He had done the impossible, gone to hell and back, and it had all been for naught. Tears flooded his eyes as his hands clenched into fists. The most intense pain drilled through his chest. The doctor's voice came from afar.

"I'm very sorry for your loss."

The doctor kept talking, but Roger couldn't hear anything else.

SLOTH

Oliver found a place to park pretty easily. This particular weeknight, the hospital appeared to have little to no activity, with only a few cars sprinkled throughout the parking lot. Oliver took a quick glance at his cellphone. No word from Jessica. He decided to ring her.

The line rang for a few seconds before she picked up.

"I'm here," he said.

"Where?"

"In the parking lot. This place is huge. Where am I supposed to see you?"

"I'm in the east wing of the building. Where are you?"

"I don't fucking know," he replied, irritated and looking frantically for a sign.

"Alright, relax. I'll walk around the hospital. Flash your headlights when you see me, okay?"

"Cool." He hung up.

Oliver waited for several minutes. He had chewed off almost all of his nails by the time he saw a shadow walking by in front of him. Her hoodie covered her almost entirely. Even though he couldn't see her perfectly, the way she walked was a dead giveaway.

He did as he was told and flashed the headlights. The figure turned around and walked in his direction, her arms wrapped around her body. Oliver opened the doors. Jessica sat in the passenger seat and rubbed her hands on her face. She looked as if she'd stayed awake for a whole week, her eyes swollen. She took a deep breath and locked her gaze with his.

"I'm glad to see you're okay," she said.

"Same."

She reached for her pocket and placed a cellphone on the dashboard.

"You think you can unlock this thing?"

Oliver grabbed it and inspected it. It was an old Android model. The screen was cracked in the middle, and the surface was sticky. He opened his mouth but figured it was better not to ask too many questions. He figured there was nothing to lose by trying what he'd learned from his cousin.

Oliver pressed the on and volume button at the same time and held them, stopping as soon as he saw a blue line of text appear on the screen. Several options appeared. He chose the corresponding one using the volume key, and the phone rebooted, displaying the phone company's logo. After a few seconds, the home screen manifested.

"You could give Envy a run for his money," Jessica joked.

Oliver cracked a smile. "It ain't a big deal. It's the kind of shit on the manual that nobody reads."

"Look up the GPS."

"What's on the GPS?"

"The guy's address."

"Whose phone is this?" Oliver was already stressed enough as it is. If she had something planned, he wanted to be in on it. "What's the deal here?"

"I took it from the man who tried to kill me," she said matter-of-factly.

Oliver's eyes widened. Jessica placed her hand on his.

"I need you to trust me, Oliver. Whoever's behind this knows all of us. The more we can find out about the other people involved, the closer we'll be to catching him. One of us has to stay here at the hospital to find out more about the others. The other one will have to go to this man's address and learn as much as possible about him. Don't take it personally, but I don't think you can blend in here, so it'd be better if I stay."

"What if it's a trap?"

Jessica shook her head. "I don't think Envy wanted me to survive that encounter. But, if he's as smart as he seems, then he may have a contingency plan. Besides, this is the only lead we have." She browsed through the gallery on her phone, going back years to the only picture she had of her ex. She had kept it in case she needed to use it, and this situation merited it. "You see this man? Memorize his face. His name is Stephen Ross. If you ever bump into him or see anyone who remotely resembles him, call the cops and get the fuck away from him. You understand what I'm saying?"

Oliver squinted. The man was tanned with a gruff beard. The resolution was shit, and there were barely any distinguishable features. "Who's he?"

"Do you understand what I'm saying?" Jessica repeated. Her eyes on fire.

"Yeah, goddamn, I do. Dangerous motherfucker. I got it. Who's he?"

"My ex."

"Tch, of course he is."

"Here," she grabbed a set of keys and a wallet and placed them in Oliver's hand. "I also took this from the man who attacked me. Get inside his apartment, do your thing, and get out. Call me as soon as you find something out, okay? I'm running out of battery, so you'll have to be concise. We're close, Oliver. We're really fucking close."

Before he could utter another word, Jessica hopped out of the vehicle and scurried back to the hospital.

Oliver sat there in silence, the cold sweat from his hands sticking to the wheel. There wasn't much to it. The hacker wasn't going to stop, regardless of Oliver's allegiance. He had reached rock bottom, and there was no coming back from this, not after killing a man. The only thing that was left to do was to get rid of the son of a bitch who had turned his life into a living hell.

LUST

Jessica wasn't exactly thrilled about what she was planning. After all, she wasn't the type to ask for favors, and she wasn't going to ask for a small favor, either. She strode past the reception and went to the hallway. Even if it took her the whole night and she had to search every inch of the building, she would find Jackie.

Before Jessica climbed the figurative stairs in her life as an escort, she used to work with a group of girls she was really close with. All of them had hopes and dreams of the future, but only two of them had taken the paths they wanted. Jessica found the more upscale clientele to eventually save enough to live off her investments and study business, and Jackie found her passion when she was admitted as a nurse in the Saint-Mary Hospital. The petite, bright-smile girl was the only one with who Jessica had stayed in contact, and while they were not as close as they once were, they usually chatted every once in a while and posted on each other's social media pages.

What Jessica had in mind was not a walk in the park, and it could land Jackie in serious trouble, but then again, she could also get in trouble if the staff were to find out about her past. Jessica felt sick in the stomach just thinking about blackmailing someone who was once such a close friend, but if it came to it, then she didn't have much of a choice.

Jessica tapped on the shoulder of one of the nurses.

"Excuse me, do you know where I can find Jackie Grendwald? I'm late for my shot, and the receptionist told me to look for her."

The nurse seemed a bit taken aback. "The receptionist told you that?" She sighed. "That damn Darwin, always avoiding to do his job. Jackie should be in room eight at the end of the hall, so you can wait for her there."

"Thank you so much."

With a smile, the nurse nodded and went on her way. Jessica followed her instructions and waited outside the room. A short, young nurse with a pixie haircut stepped out of the room; she shot a quick glance at Jessica and smiled before stopping to do a double-take. Her eyes widened as she recognized her old friend.

"Oh, my God, Jessie!" she exclaimed in excitement as she gave Jessica a quick hug. "What's up? What're you doing here?"

"He's back," Jessica replied dryly.

Jackie tilted her head, visibly confused. "Who's back?"

"Remember Stephen? Remember what I told you about him that night that we . . . uh, hung out?"

The smile on Jackie's face faded in an instant. Her voice lowered to a whisper.

"No way! Wait, did you call the police?"

"No. I-I can't. It's hard to explain, but . . . it's just going to get me into much more trouble. And right now, I'm in deep shit. A friend of mine just died and—"

"Wow, hey! Stop right there. What're you telling me?"

Jessica brushed the hair out of her face and tried to sound as calm as she could. "Listen, I've done some shit, okay? Stuff I'm not proud of. Stuff that Stephen knows and—"

"So what?" Jackie exclaimed. "That was years ago. He probably doesn't have any proof of it. You can't let him bully you."

"Jackie, please. You don't understand, and I don't have much time to explain. Maybe I had a chance of taking him off my back before, but I was scared shitless, and I just made things worse. Right now, the only way to stop him is by finding whoever is responsible for trying to ruin my life."

Jackie stood bewildered. She raised her hand.

"Jess, you're not making any sense right now. But how about we talk this over after my shift?"

"I can't wait that long, and I know that you're busy. I just need a huge favor."

Jackie stepped back. "What kind of favor?"

"I need you to spare me one of your uniforms and maybe your card."

"Jess, I can't do that. Not only could I lose my job, but I would never be able to get another one. And you would surely go to jail for impersonating a nurse."

"I'm not going to interact with anybody. I just need to access a few records, and I'll be out of your life forever if that's what you want."

"I'm sorry, but the answer is no, Jessica."

Jackie turned around, headed in the opposite direction.

"You know, it'd be a shame if people found out about your former job," Jessica shouted.

Jackie stopped. She glanced over her shoulder, shooting Jessica a ravenous look. She walked over to Jessica, her eyes red bloodshot, and watery. Jackie's lips trembled as she whispered.

"I can't believe you'd go so low. I thought we were friends." She shoved her card in Jessica's hand and closed it in a fist. "Locker room, 38. The password is 2213. Do what you have to do and bring everything back before you leave. If anything goes south, I'll report your ass to the police."

Jessica watched as Jackie stormed out with tears, now dropping down her cheeks. Jessica let out a deep sigh.

I'm sorry, Jackie. I have to do this.

Jessica lowered her gaze as she headed to the locker room. The uniform was a couple of sizes too small but still fit her without looking weird. Jessica then walked through the hallways of the hospital, looking for a terminal she could access.

Five minutes passed before she saw a nurse instructing one of the doctors to check on the patient. The doctor entered the room, and the nurse punched a few commands into the portable terminal. Jessica trotted toward the man. A quick glance at his ID revealed the nurse's name was Hurk.

"Hey, excuse me. Are you Hurk?"

The nurse looked straight out of college, with a chiseled face and pearl white teeth. "Uh, yeah, and you are?"

"Reception is looking for you. They said it is urgent."

Hurk looked confused. "For what?"

Jessica shrugged. "I don't know. Darwin didn't go into detail. He just wanted to see you there ASAP."

The man rolled his eyes. "Darwin. Shoulda figured."

"I can take care of this for you," Jessica offered as she pointed to the terminal.

"Thanks," Hurk smiled. "Just punch in the patient's info real quick and leave it outside room 3. I'll be right back."

Jessica winked. "You got it."

She pretended to type as the young man hurried to the stairs. Once he was out of sight, she took the terminal to a secluded area. She flattened her back against the wall to make sure nobody peeked over her shoulder. Jessica cracked her knuckles.

"Alright, who should I search for first?"

SLOTH

The place Oliver arrived at wasn't an apartment; it was a house. A decent neighborhood, as well. While Oliver didn't think this guy was exactly rich, he was definitely well off. The first key he tried was the correct one. He took a quick glance over his shoulder to make sure nobody was around before heading in.

The place was spotless, with not a single trace of dust or clutter. It was too perfect, like a dollhouse. There were no portraits, no paintings, no family photos, not even a hint of personality. The atmosphere was ominous, and the silence was deafening. He patted his hip for reassurance, but the gun wasn't there.

Fuck, I left it in the car. What a fucking idiot. Screw it. Whoever lived here is not a problem anymore.

Despite his rationale, Oliver couldn't help but feel defenseless. Even if nobody was there, the last thing he needed was to be vulnerable. Especially considering the events that had unfolded in just a couple of hours.

Got a gun pointed at my head twice and have seen more people die today than many people in their lifetimes. But hey, let's leave the gun in the car before heading to a maniac's house.

He considered going back to the car but figured it would be better not to attract too much attention. All it would take was one neighbor to be looking outside at the wrong time to get caught. Although, if he had the key to the house, was it really a break-in?

Oliver ignored those thoughts as he stopped in the middle of the living room. A set of clothes was folded neatly on the sofa. He unfolded it and searched through the pockets. He found a bit of change and a card from Costco. It had the name Trevor Bates on it and a picture. It was the clown.

Oliver's blood turned cold. His heartbeat quickened as he tried to understand what was happening. It couldn't be the same man that had tried to kill Jessica. No, she had dealt with one psycho and Oliver with another. Could it be that they were together on it? It wasn't too far-fetched, considering how Oliver, Jessica, and Timothy knew each other. Maybe this was a similar situation. In that case, then Jessica was right. Perhaps all the people that Envy had hacked were connected after all.

Oliver reached for his phone but stopped. Perhaps, it'd be better to call Jessica once he had more info. Right now, he just had one name and confirmation that they knew each other. His gut told him there was more to the story.

The smell of a nice beef stew flooded his nostrils. And damn, did it smell good. He figured a quick look around the kitchen could bring some answers too.

The kitchen looked as impeccable as the rest of the house, with a lonely pot steaming on the cooktop. Oliver stepped closer and inhaled the fumes. It was amazing. His stomach growled in protest. Following his instincts, he grabbed a spoon and took a sip of the stew. Not bad at all, but it tasted a bit funny. Even though it looked to be beef, the texture and flavor were more akin to pork. Oliver shrugged it off and left the spoon where he found it.

He reached out to the fridge and opened it. Oliver hopped back, almost tripping over his own feet. His face contorted into a grimace as he tried to cover his nose with his hands. He could feel his skin crawling as he took in every detail of the gruesome scene.

Wrapped inside plastic laid a mutilated hand. Long, delicate and polished nails revealed that it belonged to a woman, a lonely engagement ring still attached to one of the fingers. Blood oozed out of a cut in the plastic. The small stain led to a trail down the wall of the fridge that had turned brown.

Oliver felt like he was going to vomit. He managed to swallow back his lunch and slammed the fridge shut. He tilted his head upward and closed his eyes as he tried to recompose.

What the fuck, man. What the flying fuck

Just when he thought he had pulled himself together, the doorbell rang, startling him. This was bad. If someone were to catch him there, not only trespassing but next to somebody's corpse, then he'd be in some serious shit. Oliver started hyperventilating, the weight of his clothes heavy like armor.

Relax, just relax. Just play it off.

Against better judgment, Oliver decided to do what he had done all night, the only thing that had kept him alive for so long: follow his gut.

He looked through the peephole and swallowed. There was an old lady, at least the top portion of her head. She was so short that he could barely see her eyes.

"Matty, are you there?" she asked. "Don't hide from me. I can see your shadow from under the door."

Oliver cursed to himself. "Sorry, lady. Whatever you're selling, we ain't buying."

"Oh, no. I'm Matty's neighbor. You must be the date he was talking about."

Date! That's it!

"Yeah, uh, sorry, but we're not exactly decent at the moment."

The woman jerked her head back in surprise. "Oh, I'm sorry, dear. I was just walking by and recognized the smell of Matty's delicious stew. You can smell that from the other side of the street! Oh, well, I'll be on my merry way. I hope I didn't interrupt anything."

Lady, just the fuck shut up and leave!

Finally, the lady turned around and walked down the steps of the porch. Oliver let out a sigh of relief. He saw her disappear into the night. He opened the door slightly and peeked out; his ear lifted in the direction she had taken. Not a sound.

He closed the door again and resumed his search. The rest of the house seemed ordinary, plain even. Save for the severed human limb just hanging out in the kitchen, there wasn't anything else worth pointing out. The man didn't seem to have any close relatives. And based on what the lady had said, the man seemed to be gay, or at least bisexual. No indication of a serious relationship. The only clothes in the closet seemed to be of the same size, so it was safe to assume it all belonged to the owner of the house.

There was still one place he needed to inspect, and Oliver had saved it for last for a reason. The truth was that he was scared shitless.

He didn't want to go any further into the rabbit hole, but he had to. If there was anything he was more afraid of than dying, it was losing his family. He couldn't bear the thought of never seeing his aunt nor his cousins ever again. Even if it cost him everything, making sure they were alive and well was the only choice he had.

Oliver stood in front of the door to the basement. He turned the knob and was met with a set of creaking stairs leading down to a black void. He groped the wall to the side, found the light switch, and turned it on. The place was flooded by a yellow light. Unlike the rest of the house, it looked like a mess.

There was litter on the floor, mountains of stuff cluttered the space to the corners of the room, and a huge red stain spread all over the floor as if somebody had grabbed a bucket of paint and emptied it. Oliver walked down slowly, his mind screaming for help with each step as his heart throbbed. Once he reached the end, his jaw opened wide.

There was a wooden chair in the middle of the room with a half-naked man tied to it. The naked man's eyes gazed down at the ground, inert and lifeless. The tone of his skin was a sickening gray, and his right arm and left leg were missing, only a red stomp of torn flesh in their respective places.

Oliver stood paralyzed, mesmerized by the horrific scenery. His pocket started to vibrate, and he answered the call without looking, his eyes fixed on the corpse.

"H-Hello?"

"Oliver, you're not going to believe this." Jessica's voice was a welcoming surprise. He felt better even if she wasn't there with him. "What I found is . . . unbelievable. It's all starting to make sense."

"What're you on about?"

"There was an accident years ago. A huge car crash. Wait, before I explain, let me ask. Did you find anything?"

"A name." Oliver's voice was shaky. He tried to sound as calm as possible, but the corpse decomposing right in front of him wasn't helping. "The man who was supposed to kill me, his name was Trevor Bates. I think he knew the man who attacked you."

"Holy shit. We're onto something. Did you find anything else?"

Oliver turned to the corpse and remembered the hand in the fridge. "I-I don't think you'll want to know the details."

"Well, listen to this. The man Envy sent to kill me is called Matthew Walker. He's a nurse at the Saint-Mary Hospital. He attended to the victims of the accident back then. Timothy talked about it on the news when it happened. There were several victims. A woman and her daughter, Diana, and Elizabeth Bates . . ."

"Wait, that's the last name of—"

"Yes," Jessica assured. "Trevor was the only survivor of his family. Apparently, he's been in and out of the hospital every once in a while due to bar fights. Ex-military."

Oliver rubbed his head. "Fuck, man . . ."

"Apparently, a drunk truck driver was responsible for the crash. Brian Thompson. I thought the name sounded familiar, so I looked him up. He's been missing for the last couple of days."

Oliver landed his eyes on the corpse before him. Could it be?

"I think I found him."

"What are you talking about?"

"There's a . . . uh, a dead body in the basement. He's really fucked up."

"Well . . . uh, that's one suspect off the list, I guess," Jessica said. "There's another survivor. A lone driver by the name of Roger Johnson who only had a few scratches and bruises."

"Dunno anything about him."

"There's another lady admitted right now under the same surname. I'll talk to her."

"Sounds good."

"There was another couple that died," Jessica continued. "A man and his wife. The kid who was with them survived but suffered serious injuries. He ended up in a wheelchair for the rest of his life."

Oliver swallowed. The story was starting to sound too familiar. "Jess . . ."

"Oliver . . . there's something I need to ask you."

"Don't. Please, don't . . ."

"Oliver, what's your last name?"

Oliver lowered his gaze and tried to hold back the tears. "Please, don't tell me."

"It's Grant, isn't it?" Jessica finally asked.

The name pierced in his ears like a dagger. "Yes."

Jessica sighed. "The couple who died. Those were your parents? And the little kid was your cousin, wasn't it?"

Oliver started to sob. His face contorted and reddened as he realized what it all meant.

"This ain't happening," Oliver let out. "This ain't happening . . ."

There was silence on the other end of the line. He clenched the phone tightly to his ear. He could barely listen to her breathing.

"Don't say it," Oliver begged. "Don't you fucking say it."

"You said Freddy is pretty tech-savvy, isn't he?"

"Jessica, I'm going to hang up the phone if you don't shut the fuck up right now," Oliver threatened. "You realize what you're saying? Because you don't know him like I do, he would never . . ."

"You said he's changed since the accident."

"He's a fucking cripple!" Oliver yelled. "Of course he's changed! But he took it like a champ! He's a fighter! He's not a coward who hides behind a keyboard, playing fucking mind games."

There was a long pause. Oliver waited for Jessica's response.

"Okay," she finally said. "Let's not get ahead of ourselves. There's still this Roger guy. Come back to the hospital, and we'll figure this out together."

Oliver wiped off his face with his sleeve. "I'll see you there."

GREED

Roger Johnson sat in the hospital's waiting room, expressionless, his eyes fixed on nothing at all. His mind was whirling with a thousand different thoughts, some optimistic, some pessimistic, all contradictory. There was no pain in his heart anymore, only a void in its place. He thought about the woman who had always been there for him. The one who used to wake him up in the mornings with the smell of pancakes impregnating the house when he was a kid. The one who taught him how to ride a bike and would get worried sick every time he went out with his friends. The one who had helped him pay rent in his darkest days. The one who'd visit him every once in a while with homemade food and wholesome energy. The one who had gotten older yet sweeter over the years.

There was nobody else in his life to care for. His father had left them before Roger could even remember him. Without a wife or children, Roger had always found pride in thinking of himself as a lone wolf, tied to nobody, but the truth was different. There was one person who meant the world to him. And while in hindsight it was inevitable, he never stopped to even consider what to do when he'd eventually outlive his mother.

The day had come, and all he knew was that he didn't want to feel alone anymore.

Roger's fingers slid on his scalp. He raised his head to see two nurses talking, and one of them pointed toward him. The other one thanked her and strode in his direction. Roger let out a grunt. The paperwork, the arrangements, the bills that had to be paid. Couldn't they let a man grieve in peace?

"Hello," the pretty nurse said. "Are you Mr. Roger Johnson?" Roger nodded. "Good, I'm Jess . . . I mean, Jackie. My name's Jackie. I . . . uh, I'm very sorry for your loss. I went to check on Mrs. Johnson, and they told me what happened. I know this must be very hard for you, but there are some questions I need to ask you."

"Just get it over with," Roger whispered.

The nurse looked down. "I, uh, a few years ago, you were involved in a car accident and admitted to this hospital . . ."

"What does this have to do with anything?"

The nurse seemed shaken. "I-It's just routine. Double-checking your medical history to see that everything is in order."

Roger raised an eyebrow. "Whatever."

Jackie sat beside him. "Okay, did you have any lasting effects on your health from the accident? Some sort of trauma? Nightmares?"

Roger shrugged. "I'm fine. That was a long time ago, and I just got a few scratches. And I already paid for that visit. Thank you very much. Five hundred dollars just to tell me to get painkillers."

"I'm just trying to make sure that you're doing better. So, next question. Did you know any other people from the accident?"

"You don't care. People like you don't want me to be healthy because you leech on the sick and the miserable. Nobody cares.

Everybody is out for themselves, and that's fair enough, but everybody has someone to look after or someone that is looking after them. What do I have left? Nothing."

Jackie looked extremely uncomfortable now. That was good. Everybody should get a good look at themselves every once in a while. Stand in the mirror and meet eye to eye with the pieces of shit that they are.

"Mr. Johnson, don't think like that. We all have . . . something or someone."

"Not me. Not anymore. So what's the point of it all?" Roger stood up. The nurse imitated him.

"Mr. Johnson, please, I know this isn't the best time, but I just need five minutes of your time."

"That's how it goes. Everybody always wants something from me. Everybody except her. You don't deserve my time. Nobody does."

Without saying another word, Roger turned around and headed for the emergency stairs. He wasn't in a hurry, but he walked at a brisk pace. The thumping sound behind him made him turn over his shoulder. The nurse was trying to keep up.

"Roger, you don't understand," she muffled, out of breath. Now that he took a closer look at her, there were bags under her eyes, and skin seemed paler than what it should have been. Long shift, probably.

"Look, I'm sorry, but I don't care. Just leave me alone."

He opened the door to the stairs and went up, skipping two steps at the time. Jackie followed. Roger reached the last set of stairs while the nurse begged him to come back. He slammed the door open with his arm. Clouds almost entirely covered the night sky; only the silhouette of the moon could be seen between the shades of gray.

Roger stopped dead on his tracks and took it all in. The lights of the city sparkled brightly from afar. The chilly breeze made the hairs on his body stand on end. Never in his life had he really stopped to notice the small details, those that make you feel alive. It was ironic that he noticed them now, considering his intentions.

The door opened behind him. Roger ignored it and took a few slow steps toward the edge of the rooftop.

"Wow, hey! Roger, what're you doing?" the nurse shouted.

"Stop pretending to care. Leave. Tell your boss or a doctor that you saw a man jump from the roof, and you couldn't stop it. Cry if you have to. Nobody is going to judge you. You don't have to stay and watch."

She tried to grab him by the shoulder. Roger avoided her hand and climbed on top of the stone ledge. She stopped with her hands raised in surrender.

"If you take another step, I'll jump," Roger said calmly. "I don't want to have an audience, so I would like you to leave. Now."

"Roger, please. This isn't the answer. Just talk to me, okay?"

"I'm tired of talking. I'm tired of it all. If you knew the things I've done, you'd leave in utter disgust."

"My name's not Jackie!" the nurse exclaimed. "My name's Jessica. I'm a prostitute. I've done horrible stuff too, Roger. I've taken drugs, I've sold drugs, I've lied, I've blackmailed, I've killed." Roger was ready to call bullshit on her, but as tears filled her eyes, he realized she was telling the truth. "I was never a good daughter. My mom raised me all by herself and sacrificed everything, and I abandoned her. I ran away with a maniac who would hit me, rape me, torture me, and make me feel like shit. And now, the only time in my whole fucking life where I feel that I finally have some fucking control. When I've found something remotely close to happiness, some asshole tells my ex where I am and . . ." She lowered her head. "And I don't think I can take it anymore. But I'm going to fight until the end."

Roger stood in silence. Yes, she sounded like a broken person, but she still had that drive to live, to get out on top. He didn't. The last flame of his will to live extinguished the moment he heard about his mother's passing.

"I killed her . . ." Roger whispered. "It's my fault she died. If only I would've done as she said. If only I had gone to college like she said, or if I had met someone, I would've had the money for her treatment. She would still be alive. I tried my best. God knows that. I did all I could to save her. Even going so far as to take a life . . ."

A ubiquitous silence engulfed the hospital's rooftop, only the whistling of air present.

"Who was it?" Jessica asked, more serene but with tears sliding down her cheeks. "Whoever it was, I'm sure you had a reason. I'm sure it's because there was no other way. I killed someone, too, Roger. In self-defense, but it doesn't make me feel any better."

"I didn't," said Roger. "The man I killed was the head of a family. I made a woman into a widow and kids without a father. He didn't attack me. I broke into his home and killed him in front of them. The way she screamed when she saw him fall was the most heart-wrenching sound I've ever heard. It'll haunt me for eternity. I know why I did it, and I would do it again if it meant saving her, but it was all for naught. The only person who truly loved me is gone, and I have no one to blame but myself for that."

"And this is your solution?" Jessica asked, taking one step closer, her hands rising slowly in the air. "Think about it. You really think this is what she would've wanted?"

Roger shrugged. "It doesn't matter what she would've wanted. She's dead. I've never been really religious, but I always thought there was . . . something or someone up there. I mean, there had to be. Someone who would make things right. But now that I'm looking at death right in the eyes, I realize that she's gone for good. She's not looking down from above, waiting for me. No. There's no life after this one. Just . . . darkness. People of faith have something to look forward to. Even in mourning, there's hope. A certainty that they're going to see their loved ones in the afterlife, but I don't have that."

"That's more of a reason not to jump!" Jessica shouted, only a couple of steps away from Roger. "If there's no life after this one, then you have to live your life to the fullest."

"What's a life without a smile?" Roger asked calmly. "If there's nobody there for you to count on and support. Whatever enjoyment I can ever find after this is going to be clouded knowing that she's no longer here with me."

Jessica now stood at his feet. "You know, you're right. Maybe there's no life after this one. Maybe there's no meaning to all of this, and there's no reason to stay alive. But she's not gone. She lives in your memory. You're the only one left in this world who's ever going to cherish those moments when she was alive. If you die, then she truly is gone."

A faint smile drew on Roger's somber face. "Thank you. Really. Thank you for trying. But I'm afraid it's not enough."

He took one step forward.

"No!" she screamed.

"This is the only way to make the pain go away forever."

Roger raised his arms to the side and dropped into the void. He felt the rising sense of vertigo on his belly as the air brushed his face and hair. For a split second, he was flying, free of all pain, free of restrictions. The concrete floor below rushed toward him.

He closed his eyes.

The most intense pain ran from the top of his head to the tip of his toes as his skull crashed into the pavement, but as soon as it came, it was gone.

Then, there was nothing.

SLOTH

Oliver froze at the entrance to the hospital. It was him, the man Jessica had warned him about. Stephen Ross. A tall, brick of a man with tanned skin, ragged clothes, an unkempt beard, and bloodshot eyes. Even from afar, the foul smell emanating from Stephen hit Oliver's nostrils, making him frown.

Stephen was shouting at the receptionist. Oliver sneaked his way through without taking his eyes off the man. The scars of his face and erratic eyes made him look like a mad man.

Once Oliver had safely retreated to one of the hospital's hallways, he reached for his phone and called Jessica. The line rang for a couple of minutes, but there was no answer. He kept trying, afraid that her battery had already run out, but to no avail.

After scanning the entire second floor and several calls forwarded to voicemail, Oliver finally saw Jessica's name turn green on the phone.

"Hello?" she sounded muffled, like she'd been crying.

"Hey, man, you okay?" Oliver asked.

"I'm . . . alive . . . Where are you?"

"Your psycho ex is here."

"What?!" Jessica yelled. "Oliver, you have to get the fuck out of here!"

"Yeah, no shit. I ain't leaving without you, though. Where you at?"

"I'm on the roof . . ."

"What'cha you doing up there? Are you stargazing at a time like this?"

"It doesn't matter now. I'll be going down. Meet me on the ground floor, near the ER."

"Got it." He hung up.

Oliver was already on the ground floor, so it didn't take him long to reach the emergency room. He stood near the entrance. A nurse stopped to ask him if he needed anything, and he just shrugged her off. One minute passed, then two minutes. Time seemed to slow to a halt. Despite the air conditioning operating at full capacity, Oliver was sweating buckets. It was then that it occurred to him. How did the hacker know where to send Jessica's ex? Either he'd been listening, or he was tracking their phones.

Oliver reached into his pocket and gave a long, last look at his cell. It wasn't the fanciest model, and with a cracked screen and shitty interface, he was pretty sure he could find something better for cheap. Oliver threw it in a nearby trashcan and waited. Finally, he saw Jessica arrive. She was wearing scrubs.

"The hell took you so long?" Oliver asked.

"Had to take the stairs."

He grabbed her hand and dragged her out through the hallways of the hospital.

"We should call the cops."

"What?" she tried to jerk her hand free but couldn't. "We can't do that, Oliver. We're so close to getting him. It's just going to slow us down at this point."

"Exactly. I'm not saying we should stay put for them. Let's just call them and beat it. Let your ex handle them."

They turned on a corner.

"Oliver, I'm sure I know who the hacker is."

They stopped in their tracks. Oliver stared at the end of the hallway. All the way to the back, the elevator doors opened. Stephen Ross stepped out.

Jessica's hand was gripping Oliver's so tightly that it hurt. Oliver tried to drag her, but she was planted on the floor like a pillar. He lowered his hand and intertwined his fingers with hers. She turned to Oliver, and he gave her a reassuring nod.

Stephen set an eye on them. His glare was that of pure, maniacal rage. Oliver pulled Jessica, and she followed suit. They dashed through the hallways of the hospital. Oliver looked over his shoulder to see Stephen running toward them at full speed, knocking over everything and everyone in his path. Jessica tried to call for help, but out of her mouth came only a whimper. As they reached the lobby, Oliver was the one to gather enough courage to shout:

"Security! Somebody call security!"

The automatic double doors slid open. Jessica and Oliver pushed a man out of their way to the exit. The couple zigzagged their way through the cars of the parking lot as rain sprinkled on them.

"Where's the gun?" she asked in a mixture of exhaustion and desperation.

"In the car," Oliver replied. He pulled the car keys out and pressed the button.

A beep echoed in the distance. They headed in that direction. Oliver pressed the button again. This time, he saw a blink of orange and red in the distance. His legs screamed in pain, and he felt as if his lungs were about to burst out of his chest.

They finally reached the car. Oliver inserted the key in the door. The next thing he knew, he was on the ground, his head banging against the concrete. Jessica burst out a scream. He had been tackled.

Stephen was on top of him; the man's massive body had Oliver almost completely immobilized. Both of Stephen's hands wrapped around Oliver's neck and squeezed. Jessica stood with her eyes open wide and both hands on her mouth. She was shaking all over. Oliver wished he could scream and tell her to go away, or fight the guy, anything. His lips managed to wheeze out a single word:

"Gun . . ."

Jessica seemed to wake from her trance, finally snapping back to reality and the situation settling in her head. She opened the car and dove inside. Oliver tried to take Stephen's hand off his neck, but his efforts were futile. He could feel that the taste of his tongue had grown sour as he tried to gasp for air. His eyes contorted back, almost welcoming the darkness.

"Stop, or I'll shoot!" He heard from afar, like an echo from a cave.

Stephen turned around as his grip loosened, enough for Oliver to finally take in some air. He felt his lungs burning and his throat throbbing. Oliver started to cough as he watched the events unfold like he was in some sort of dream.

"You grew some balls," Stephen hissed.

Stephen released his grip and rose to his feet, turning to face Jessica. Oliver felt as if he was about to spit out his lungs. Jessica held the gun high, her hands shaking but her aim firm.

"I'm not fucking around, Stephen," Jessica threatened.

"I remember when you used to shit yourself every time you saw me."

"I'm not that little girl anymore." Her voice cracked, and her eyes shone brightly. She wasn't going to give him the satisfaction of crying. Never again.

"Oh, but you still are." Stephen stepped closer. "You got fat and fake tits, but you're the same piece of shit I picked up from her mother's basement. Someone was going to try and sell you eventually. If it wasn't me, it was going to be your crack whore of a mother for some spare change. At least, with me, you got a profit. I gave you freedom."

"Freedom? Fucking freedom? I was your prisoner."

"You loved me."

"Stockholm syndrome is one hell of a ride."

Stephen took a quick glance at the gun, smirking.

"You wouldn't dare."

"Stay the fuck away."

Oliver tried to pull himself together. Still coughing, he stumbled back up to his feet. His hand gently rubbed his neck.

"C'mon, baby, I know you still go crazy for me," Stephen said with a wide grin on his face.

"I do. Just not the way you imagine."

Stephen raised his hands as if surrendering. Jessica's finger hovered over the trigger. Stephen glanced at Oliver from the corner of his eye. Before either of them could react, Stephen stepped back and grabbed Oliver with a swift movement, grappling him from the back. Stephen now had Oliver as a human shield with his arm pressed tightly on Oliver's throat.

"Put the gun down," Stephen ordered. Jessica stayed still, her eyes switching from Oliver to Stephen.

Shoot, Jessica, Oliver thought, wanting to scream. *C'mon, girl, take the shot.*

Oliver could feel his heart racing. Jessica was considering her options. She was trying to see if she could land the shot on Stephen's head. Oliver was positive that she could but was also aware that even the tiniest mistake could kill him.

"You've always been a cocky motherfucker," Jessica spat. "You think nothing gets past you. That you have everything under control, that's how I tricked you back then. Making you believe that you had complete control over me. And look how it turned out. Almost seventeen years later, and you still believe that lie."

Stephen squeezed harder. Oliver let out a whimper. "You're testing your luck, bitch. If you don't want to see the kid die, drop the fucking gun."

Jessica took a deep breath. She raised her hands, the gun now pointing upward to the sky.

"I won't shoot," she said. "Let him go."

"Put the gun on the ground."

"Stephen . . ."

"Put the fucking gun on the ground, you bitch! Or I'll snap his fucking neck!"

Jessica knelt, her eyes fixed on her ex-boyfriend. She placed the gun on her feet and rose back up.

"Kick it," he ordered.

She obeyed. The gun ended up on Stephen's feet. He pushed Oliver aside. Oliver's head bumped into the car with a bang. Stephen picked up the gun and pointed it at them.

"Get in the car," Stephen growled. "Both of you."

With a grimace, Oliver rubbed his head where he had been hit, walked over to the passenger seat, and entered. Jessica headed to the back seat. Stephen raised his hand to stop her.

"No, bitch. You're driving."

LUST

With Oliver in the passenger seat and Stephen sitting in the back with a gun pointed at her head, Jessica could only keep her eyes on the road. She clutched the wheel, her nails digging into the leather. This was madness. She had been driving for several minutes with no clear directions. Every once in a while, Stephen would tell her to take a right, a left, an exit, and so forth. It felt like they were going in circles, but she was sure that Stephen had a destination in mind.

They took the highway. Judging by the dry mountains manifesting around them, they were leaving the city. Not too long after, the buildings started to grow fewer and farther from each other. Miles of dead, barren land stretched as far as the eye could see, engulfed by darkness.

Jessica made a conscious effort to memorize the route, thinking of a way to escape the situation. At the moment, there didn't seem to be a way out that wouldn't potentially kill or injure one of them. She had dragged Oliver into her mess, and she wasn't going to let him die because of her. Jessica had already seen too many people die that night, two of which she couldn't save.

She glared at the dashboard. They had less than a quarter of a tank. Depending on how far Stephen was taking them, they would eventually have to stop at a gas station. And there was no way Stephen would dare to fire a gun in a gas station, risking blowing them all up to pieces.

However, her ex was psychotic enough to do some crazy shit. A lot of time had passed since she last saw him, and time hadn't been kind to him, so who knew. Maybe he was capable of killing himself if it meant getting rid of her.

A road sign flew past them. Jessica had time to steal a fleeting glance. She had an idea as to where they were headed. There was a dam nearby. More specifically, they were nearing a bridge that crossed over a river near the dam. She moved her fingers on the wheel, her hands sweaty and cold as she flirted with an idea.

Jessica turned her head to the passenger seat, and her eyes met Oliver's. His gaze was that of despair, someone on the verge of panic. She could see the exhaustion and fear in him. Jessica felt a huge urge to apologize. He had his own shit to deal with, and now they were both in the same game. Oliver could've gotten away. He didn't have to endure this ordeal. He didn't deserve it.

Her eyes watered as she thought of everything that could go wrong if she did what she was thinking. But whatever the result, it would be better than going with Stephen to the middle of nowhere where he would surely kill them both and get rid of the bodies.

As if Oliver could read her mind, he nodded. He seemed reluctant but apparently had reached the same conclusion as Jessica. With extreme caution, she took her left hand off the wheel and slid her finger down. From the corner of her eye, she saw the button that engaged the child safety lock on the doors. She pressed the button, effectively closing Stephen's way out of the car. She then slid her hand to her seatbelt. Jessica swallowed dryly as she stole a glance at the rearview mirror and met Stephen's menacing gaze. She adjusted the mirror slightly.

"Hey!" Stephen protested. "Whatcha doing?"

Jessica inhaled deeply, trying to keep cool. "I'm just trying to see what's behind me, and you're in the way."

"Don't play smart with me, bitch, or I'll blow your fucking brains out."

"I wouldn't recommend doing so while we're on the highway," she said without thinking.

"Shut the fuck up."

Stephen leaned back in his seat and out of her sight in the mirror. Jessica looked at Oliver. The boy was now staring at the window. The poor guy's lips shuddered as if he was freezing. She coughed gently. Oliver turned, and she pointed at her seatbelt, trying to form a silent phrase with her lips: "Take it off."

Oliver nodded. He reached out to the dashboard and turned on the radio.

"What the fuck, kid!" Stephen yelled, waving his gun at Oliver's head.

"Wow, hey, dude, chill! I'm just trying to relax, okay? I need some music on. I'm about to shit my pants over here."

"Don't get comfortable, punk," Stephen threatened. "This may be your last groove."

She followed the road signs like Stephen had instructed until she took an exit and stopped at a red light. The bridge stood in front of them. The moon hovered over the river with a silvery glow. The edge of the dam was clearly visible in all its splendor.

Jessica took a deep breath.

"Dude, where are you taking us?" Oliver asked.

"None of your fucking business, kid."

"It is my fucking business if I'm being kidnapped," Oliver snapped.

Oliver, please. Really a bad time to grow a pair.

"Oliver, shut up," she said.

Stephen let out a chuckle. "You heard the lady, pal. Shut your fucking mouth."

Oliver swallowed, his Adam's apple went up and down in a gulp. The sweat on his face and neck reflected the streetlights around them. Jessica saw how Oliver swiftly pressed on the release button of his seatbelt. She did the same, the click muffled by the music on the radio. A light on the dashboard blinked, signaling that she had taken off her seatbelt.

"If any of you tries to do anything funny, I swear." Stephen pressed the gun on the back of Oliver's seat. "Maybe I should just kill you, kiddo. I don't have any use for you. I got my prize right here."

"Do it then," Jessica threatened, her voice firm as stone. "Get rid of your only leverage, and I'll drive us all straight into oncoming traffic."

"Psst, whatever, honey . . . I know you aren't the tough girl you pretend to be."

"You don't know what I'm capable of. Not anymore."

"Course I do, love."

You're about to find out soon, though.

The dashboard beeped. The words "Seat Belt Not On" kept blinking sporadically and seemed to glow brighter by the second. Through the rearview mirror, she saw Stephen's confused expression as he squinted to see the dashboard. His eyes widened as he realized what was happening.

Jessica slammed the pedal. The car's engine roared to full force as the tires sped up. The three of them were pushed back by the force. Stephen pushed himself forward, his face already red, filled with rage. He tried to put the gun on Jessica's head, but she turned the wheel to the side, making them take a left to the opposite lane. Stephen stumbled to the side.

Two beams of light flashed at her, the lights coming straight at them in a matter of seconds. Jessica turned the wheel back to their lane just in time as the side of her car scraped the other one, a lingering honk leaving them behind.

The vehicle reached the bridge. Jessica headed straight to the side of the bridge without hesitation. Just before they reached the edge, she screamed at the top of her lungs:

"Jump!"

Oliver pulled the handle and slammed his shoulder against the door, but it didn't budge. Jessica did the same. She glanced over the shoulder to see Stephen kicking the door to his side hysterically.

In just a split second, Jessica realized two things. The first one was that she had focused all of her efforts into putting the child safety lock on for Stephen and taking their seat belts off without raising any suspicions from him that she forgot to open the doors as she yelled at Oliver to jump. The second one was that they were now in mid-air, the car wheels touching nothing as they plunged into the black waters below.

Miguel Estrada

SLOTH

Oliver raised his arms as he braced himself for impact. In less than a second, the bright starry sky turned into a swirling mess of waves clashing, giving the impression of amorphous shapes swimming beneath the water's surface. His body was propelled forward as the car crashed head-on into the river, an explosion of foam enveloping everything around them. His head seemed to split in half as it struck the dashboard.

Oliver struggled to make sense of what was going on as several different stimuli overwhelmed his senses. His whole body ached in pain, there was a loud buzzing in his ear, and his vision struggled to adapt to the darkness, barely able to see silhouettes and faint colors around them, the most striking of which was red. They were soaked in red.

There was something huge next to him, lying on the windshield and contorted to the side in an unnatural manner. Oliver jerked back in surprise as he realized that it was Stephen. The bastard had plummeted to the front of the car and smashed against the windshield. In the driver's seat, next to their kidnapper's unconscious body, sat Jessica. Her head was resting on the wheel with hair mangled in it and a fountain of blood and snot pouring out of her nose. Oliver tried to move, but a surge of pain ran through his limbs. He didn't know if it was a broken bone or a fatal wound and didn't care.

Oliver rose from his seat and leaned over to Jessica. He stretched out his arm, struggling to reach over Stephen. The tip of his fingers brushed against Jessica's neck. It wasn't close enough to check her pulse.

A loud crack startled him.

Oliver's eyes glued to the windshield, from where a huge crack webbed outwards from the center. His feet were numb, almost nonexistent. The sound of running water made him realize the situation he was in. He raised his feet, now aware that they were drenched. A pool of water had been slowly rising from under the seats. Water was leaking from somewhere, and he was sure that it wouldn't take long before they were submerged in it.

Everything around him turned darker by the second. Bubbles danced up from outside the window as the car sank deeper into the river. The water that had been on his ankles was now up to his knees. Oliver put his feet up on the seat and leaned to the driver's side. From up close, he could see that Jessica was still breathing.

Oliver grabbed her by the shoulders as best as he could and shook her.

"Jess! Jessica! Wake the fuck up! We need to get the fuck outta here!"

He stopped to think. There had to be a way out. His eyes scanned the inside of the car, looking desperately for something he could use. Under the black pool beneath him, he could barely make out the shape of the gun under the seat. It must've fallen out of Stephen's hand after the crash.

The water was quickly rising to his chest. He grabbed Jessica by the hair and pulled her head back before the water reached her nose.

Without wasting any more time, Oliver took a deep breath and held it. He dove in, his hand groping blindly in the dark before touching cold metal and rose back out for a deep, desperate breath. The gun was soaked. He wasn't sure if it would even fire right after being underwater. Besides, he couldn't remember how many bullets it had left, and they were all cramped inside a very small space. If anything went wrong, he could hurt himself or Jessica. He put the gun inside his pants and turned to look over his shoulder.

Oliver had heard somewhere that the reason why headrests could be detached from the seat was for people to use it as a tool in case of an emergency. He wasn't sure if it was true, but he was going to try it anyway. He had to make a conscious effort to stop his fingers from shaking as he detached the headrest.

His eyes went to Jessica once again, considering his options before proceeding. He wondered if his scrawny body would be able to lift Jessica and swim up with her. He hoped that he could. There was no way he'd let her die.

Oliver took a deep puff of air and held it. He raised his hands, the sharp end of the headrest pointing straight at the cracked windshield. As he prepared to swing, a cold hand gripped his thigh. Oliver jolted in surprise and horror as Stephen's pale hands scrambled aimlessly. Stephen grabbed Oliver's shirt, his eyes still dazed. Oliver roared at the top of his lungs, and he smashed the headrest's metal rod into Stephen's eye. The man screamed in agony as his hands fumbled to his face.

Oliver pulled the headrest back. Blood spurted out of Stephen's eye socket.

In a last-ditch effort to stay alive, Oliver struck again, but this time at the windshield. The glass shattered. Water rushed inside the vehicle. Oliver turned and grabbed Jessica by the armpits in the flash of a second. He managed to save a quick last breath as the water finally reached the car's ceiling and put Jessica's arm over him. He knelt on the seat and propelled himself forward with his feet.

Oliver swam through the windshield and out of the car, holding Jessica with both arms.

They were now floating in the middle of nowhere, surrounded by a void holding them in a cold embrace. Oliver took a quick glance over his shoulder one last time and saw the car slowly disappear into the gloom, Stephen's shadow juddering, still stuck on the windshield.

Excruciating seconds passed as he struggled to swim up. His lungs were on fire as he fought off the instinct to breathe until he could finally see beams of light dancing above him. Oliver thanked God for his mercy as the surface slowly neared.

Oliver's head sprang out of the water, his jaw wide open as he inhaled the glorious air of the night in a desperate gasp. Oliver located the nearest source of light and swam there, trying to maintain Jessica's head above the water as best as he could.

He finally reached the shore and dragged Jessica's body as far as he could from the current. His muscles ached, and his drenched clothes felt hundreds of pounds heavier. He put Jessica's head to rest on the sand and put his finger under her nose. She wasn't breathing.

"Oh, no, no, no. C'mon, girl. Don't die on me like this. You're stronger than this."

Without hesitation, he ripped her shirt open, revealing her bare chest. He pumped on her chest three consecutive times, closed her nose, and gave her some air.

He repeated the same process over and over again, just like he'd seen in class. Oliver used to always joke with his pals that he'd be the one to help them if they ever choked on their own vomit while high. They had always jested back that he would be too high to do so.

Jessica wasn't responding.

Oliver shook his head, refusing to believe that there was no hope left. He sat back, his hands reaching his face while he struggled to hold back the tears. He let out a loud, shrieking sob as his body shrank into a fetal position. The sound of the river clashing beside him dissipated.

The almost incapacitating cold he'd been feeling for the last few minutes disappeared. He simply sat there, lost and alone. He wasn't able to save her, and he wouldn't be able to save his family.

What was he going to do now? He'd have to tell everything to the police, which would surely mean his ass would end up in jail. And that was in the best of scenarios. If NV had a contingency plan for Jessica, then there would be one for Oliver as well, right? Not that it'd matter. His family was probably dead at this point. Without them, Oliver was nothing more than a scared little boy.

A strange movement caught his eye. Jessica was moving. All of a sudden, the sounds around him rushed back to life like an explosion. She was coughing her lungs out. He jumped to her and moved her sideways, where she vomited what seemed to be buckets of water.

Oliver raised her and hugged her, amazed at his miraculous feat. Jessica gently pushed him back and locked her eyes on his. The skin on her arms, knees, and thighs was scraped and glowing red. Their clothes were torn. Half of Jessica's face was full of scratches and bruises, with an open red line over her nose. Still wheezing, she spat red on the ground.

"Are you okay?" she asked as she wiped off her mouth with her sleeve.

Oliver couldn't help but let out a chuckle. "Are you really asking me if I'm okay? I should be asking you. You swallowed a shitton of water."

"Please, don't make sexual innuendo out of that."

"I can't promise anything."

She nodded. "I'm fine . . . thanks . . ."

"I need a cab," Oliver said after a pause. "I have to get going."

Jessica jerked her head back, bewildered. "Have you lost your mind?"

"He came after you. Your fucking psycho ex came after you, just like Envy said he would. Envy ain't bluffing. That means my family is still in danger. If they're not dead by now."

Oliver staggered up. Jessica grabbed his hand. "Oliver . . ."

"C'mon, Jess. If you're not coming with, then at least call me a cab. I threw away my fucking phone."

"Mine was in the car . . . And I won't leave you alone."

Sirens blared in the distance, approaching. Oliver reached out his hand to her.

"C'mon, let's get outta here."

LUST

The icy, rocky asphalt scraped against Jessica's bare feet, her legs stumbling with every other step. Her shoes hung from her fingers as she dragged herself through the decayed streets. Her whole body was soaked and in pain. This situation gave a whole new meaning to the phrase "walk of shame." Oliver strolled next to her, his somber face gazing up at the night sky. He pointed to a phone booth ahead of them.

"We can use that to call a cab," he said.

"If it still works. Besides, no one in their right minds is going to let us into their car looking like this. They'd probably call the cops on us."

"We should run then."

Jessica stopped to analyze his expression. He looked dead serious.

"I know where we are," he said. "My house is only a thirty minute walk from here."

"And you plan on walking?"

"I plan on running. It's okay if you want to leave. I don't want you to get into more trouble, but I have to see my family."

"Well, you're not going by yourself. I won't have another death on my conscience."

"Let's race then."

Despite being on the verge of exhaustion, Jessica found enough energy to push herself to run. They had to stop every couple of minutes to catch their breath.

If there was something she'd learn throughout that nightmarish ordeal, it was that she was really out of shape. Every time her thighs screamed in pain and her side ached, she remembered the video that Envy had sent Oliver. That poor old woman seemed to have such a sweet and innocent demeanor. Jessica couldn't help but feel sorry for her, imagining her in the claws of a sadistic asshole. Only God knew what kind of horrors she must've been going through at that moment if she was still alive.

Even though Jessica had trouble keeping up, the path that would otherwise have taken thirty minutes instead turned into ten minutes. They reached a rundown neighborhood. The houses were small, full of mold and garbage littering the streets, unkempt grass and the unmistakable smell of piss informed her that they were close to their destination.

Oliver stopped dead in his tracks. She stopped, too, as she tried to recover. Oliver's eyes were glued to his house.

"Something's not right," he uttered.

"How do you know?" she asked between puffs.

"My cousin's car is not here."

Jessica took a mental note of that. She didn't know exactly what time it was, but it must've been close to three or four in the morning. Where could they have gone at that time?

Oliver rushed to the porch of the house. All lights were off, except for a faint, blueish light coming from one of the bedroom's windows.

Oliver slammed the door open with his shoulder. The wooden entrance stood no chance as splinters jumped in all directions.

"Aunt Ana! Vinny!" Oliver's voice cracked with every scream. "Freddy!"

Jessica followed him. The living room was pitch black. The only source of light was the orange glow of the streetlights behind them. Oliver went to the kitchen and looked everywhere. He headed for the stairs. Jessica grabbed his arm and stopped him before he set foot on the first step.

"It's a trap, Oliver. It has to be."

Oliver snatched his arm back, his eyes shining in the darkness with a heavy air of melancholy and despair emanating from them. "I have to know."

He crept up the stairs. For the first time, Jessica no longer saw him as a scared boy but as a man. His steps were deliberate, heavy. He knew the truth, even if he didn't want to believe it. He had to see it for himself. Jessica followed Oliver up the stairs. The creaking of wood accompanied the whistling of the early morning air.

They reached the second floor. At the end of the long hallway, a white door stood closed shut. Around the frame, a halo of blue light emanated from inside.

Oliver reached inside his pants and pulled out the gun. Both of his hands gripped the weapon tightly. Jessica followed him slowly. Without even trying to turn the knob, Oliver kicked the door open.

Jessica peeked over his shoulder, and her jaw dropped the moment she saw what was inside.

SLOTH

Oliver felt the weight of the gun increase a thousandfold in his fingers. He stood there, speechless, unable to fully comprehend the situation.

They were standing at the entrance of his cousin's room, the only source of light being the three monitors of his computer, flickering a spectral white and blue shade over Freddy.

The boy sat in his wheelchair, his body contorted inward as if he was cold. He was facing them, yet one hand remained on the keyboard. His other hand was placed on the armrest of the chair. Oliver's voice shook.

"Freddy . . . where's auntie Anna? And Vinny?"

The boy only moved his eyes toward the monitors. His bony fingers began tapping on the keyboard, fast as lightning. Words materialized on the white monitors. As soon as he stopped typing, a robotic voice talked over the speakers.

"Somewhere safe."

Oliver's eyes filled with tears. "Tell me it's not what it looks like . . . please."

Jessica placed her hand on Oliver's shoulder. "I'm afraid it is."

Oliver stood paralyzed. Without realizing it, he had raised the gun. The muzzle of the weapon pointing straight at his cousin's face. His heart started beating faster as painful memories flooded into his mind. All of those horrible tasks, the painful journey he had endured. How close he'd been to death. How he had to kill a man to save his family. When in reality, the bastard responsible for everything he'd endured was part of his family all along.

His blood started to boil until he could feel his face burning with rage.

"Why?" Oliver growled.

Freddy's face remained stern as he typed.

"I think you already know the answer to that question," the robotic voice replied.

"Envy," Jessica whispered.

Freddy nodded, his face turned into a grimace as if the mere gesture caused him a great amount of pain.

"You threatened your own family!" Oliver snapped, the gun shaking in his hands. "Blood of your blood!"

"They were never in danger," the computer declared. "I can't say the same about you, cousin. You've danced with death during the last couple of days. And, to my surprise, you've come victorious."

"Victorious?" Oliver shook his head. "Is this what you think it is? A fucking game? One where you play with people's lives like they're your pawns? Huh?"

Silence reigned. It was Oliver who spoke once again. "This isn't you. You're not like this, Freddy. Someone else is making you do this, right? It's the only explanation. It has to be . . ."

"I'm afraid it's all me." The monotone sound of such a confession mixed with the rapid clattering of the keyboard gave Oliver chills. "To be honest, I never anticipated this turn of events. And believe me, I had this planned for years. Every mistake I could make, every outcome, every possibility replayed inside my mind for so long. And yet, I was unable to predict that you two would not only survive the ordeal but find the truth behind it. I had a contingency plan, yet you two came out on top once again. It's been one surprise after another all night long. I even considered involving the police, but that was out of the question. It seemed like you thought the same. It's no wonder considering the kind of stuff that you two have been up to."

"B-but . . . you're just a kid," Oliver stammered, threads of saliva glued to his lips as tears slid down his cheeks.

"I stopped being a kid years ago. That kid died along with your parents. What remains is a carcass. A broken body and soul, one that will never walk again, will never experience love or even the outside world."

"What the fuck are you on about?" Oliver screamed. "You still had a life! We walked you to the beach, to the park." He pointed to Jessica. "I even paid for a hooker for you."

"It's a life I cannot control. One that's not my own."

Oliver's gaze fell. "I knew . . . I knew you were never the same after the accident. The happy kid I grew up with, the one who would scare the shit outta me during movie nights, the one who would laugh at my bad puns. He was long gone. But I never thought I'd find a monster wearing his skin."

"I'm not the only monster in this tale," the computer said on behalf of Freddy. "We're all sinners. Everybody involved."

Oliver couldn't believe his ears. What had he ever done to gain such hatred from his dear cousin?

"What did I do to you? What did any of us do to deserve this?"

Freddy's fingers tapped faster. "You're a leech, living off other people's hard work. I can't say I'm any different, but I'm a cripple. I didn't have any choice in the matter. You, however, can choose to move out, get a real job. Instead, you lock yourself in your room all day to get high. Selling vices to kids to make ends meet and pay for more drugs. I wasn't going to allow you to live off our family. Not anymore."

Oliver took one step forward. His finger clenched on the trigger so tightly that the slightest movement could fire the gun. What hurt the most wasn't that his cousin had betrayed him, but the fact that he was telling the truth. Oliver had never done anything significant with his life. Never studied, never kept a job for more than a few months at a time. Yet, he never did anything to change that. He was comfortable. And he assumed that everybody else was too or flat out didn't care. He never stopped to consider the burden he had been to his family until after he risked losing them.

But this was just an excuse. While everything Freddy said was true, it wasn't enough of a good reason to commit such atrocities. This was just an excuse from a psychopath. Freddy was right. Oliver's innocent and happy little cousin had died years ago in that crash. What came out of the hospital was a different person altogether.

"It should've been you," Oliver finally said, his hands shaking. "It should've been you who died that night, motherfucker."

Jessica stepped over to Oliver's side.

"Please, stop," she begged. "Look around you."

Oliver turned to where she was pointing. They were barely distinguishable in the darkness, but once he saw what she meant, his heart skipped a beat. There were rows of oxygen tanks surrounding the room from all corners.

"You hear that sound?" she asked. "One of those tanks is leaking."

"So, that means . . ."

"One shot, and we all blow up to pieces."

Oliver turned to Freddy. "Was that your plan? To take us down with you? You know what. Maybe I should make your wish a reality."

Jessica stepped in between Oliver and Freddy, the gun now pointing at her chest.

"Oliver, let's get out of here. It's over."

He looked her dead in the eye. "I'm not moving until I have answers."

"You already have them. Let's leave and let the police take care of the rest."

He couldn't. As much as Oliver wanted to get out of that room and leave Freddy to rot, he couldn't just forget all of the pain. Freddy had manipulated him, tortured him, made him go through hell and back, and for what?

"You were jealous," Oliver declared in disbelief. "You were so fucking jealous of other people that you decided to destroy their lives? Tell me, was it fucking worth it?"

Freddy typed. The computer read out loud: "Every second of it."

Oliver's finger twitched. He made a supernatural effort not to shoot. Jessica's face shone in her own sweat.

"Oliver, please."

"Move," Oliver ordered.

Jessica jerked her head back in a mix of surprise and fear. She stood her ground.

"I know how you're feeling . . ."

"No, you fucking don't!"

"You're not the only one whose life has been torn apart by this asshole!" Jessica screamed. "You think I'll be the same after this? Do you think I'll be able to sleep through the night? You think I won't have nightmares about how I had to run a fucking chainsaw between a man's legs?" Jessica's eyes watered, and she did her best to avoid tearing up. "The sight of him trying to grab his own intestines to put them back is something I'll never forget. I have to live with that, same as you."

"He's my family," Oliver uttered. "But he's also this . . . thing, this monster—"

"Not just a monster," the robotic voice interrupted. "Thanks to me, a drunken piece of trash is no longer a dangerous driver on the road. A cannibalistic serial killer is no longer luring innocents to his basement. A man tormented by his past was released from his pain. The most prominent members of two gangs have been eradicated. I've purged this city from sinners."

"Bullshit," Jessica snapped as she turned over her shoulder. "You killed all of those people for the same reason you killed innocents like Timothy and Roger. You envy them. You're just looking to inflate your ego."

"That's only partially true," Freddy typed. "While my main goal has always been to ruin your lives, I realized during the planning phase that I could make the world a better place in the process."

Oliver couldn't begin to fathom the extent of everything Freddy had done. His cousin had planned every little detail. Even now, Freddy had confessed that he never anticipated Oliver and Jessica surviving and figuring out the truth.

His cousin was improvising now. Even so, knowing that he was doing exactly what Freddy wanted, Oliver couldn't help feeling tempted to pull the trigger. If it wasn't for Jessica, he would've done so already.

"You should pay for your crimes," Oliver exclaimed.

Two words manifested on all three monitors: "Do it."

Jessica raised her hands. "Oliver, think this through."

"Move," he commanded.

"No."

Oliver snatched Jessica's arm and shoved her out of the way. He took two steps forward and placed the muzzle of the gun on Freddy's forehead. The same words appeared on the screens in all caps.

"DO IT."

Oliver raised his arm and swung down, hitting Freddy on the temple with the butt of the gun. A trickle of blood slid down his cousin's neck.

"You don't deserve to die," Oliver declared. "You deserve much worse."

Oliver threw the gun into the hallway. The 9mm clashed on the floor with a loud clunk. Jessica rose to her feet, shocked and pale as a ghost.

"I thought you would . . ."

"I almost did. It took everything from me not to pull the trigger. If you weren't here, I would've done it."

Jessica sighed in relief. "Thanks for not killing us all."

"This piece of shit deserves a lifetime in prison, and that's what he'll get."

Jessica stepped closer and placed her hand on Oliver's shoulder; a tired smile drew on her face.

"Let's get out of here."

Oliver turned around, and, side by side, they both walked out of the bedroom. Midway through the hallway, the familiar typing of a keyboard manifested behind him. Oliver looked over his shoulder to see words materialize on the screen.

Red, bold letters read: "Are you sure you want to erase the hard drive? This will restore the computer to the factory settings and delete all of its content."

Freddy's finger went for the "Y" key.

"No!" Oliver yelled as he rushed back to the bedroom.

Oliver jumped, diving toward the power cord to unplug it. By the time Jessica turned to stop what was about to happen, it was too late.

What transpired after occurred in a matter of seconds. First, Freddy tapped the key. Then, Oliver hit the floor and pulled the cord out of the wall. The outlet ignited a single spark that grew wider. A bright, orange, and yellow flame engulfed all the air around the room, wrapping everything inside in a fiery wrath.

The entire house shook with the explosion, spitting a fireball through the windows and blowing out shards of glass toward the early morning sky.

JESSICA

The last thing Jessica remembered was a flash of white and yellow light. Even now, before her eyes opened, it was the only thing in her mind. That and the heat. The overwhelming heat enveloping her and swallowing her whole.

There was a beeping. Jessica couldn't place the source of the sound or even how far away it was. Someone grabbed her arm. Jessica felt the sting of a needle. It was brief, and while a little painful, it was welcomed. Any sensation was better than nothing.

She finally let her eyelids open. The light coming from above pierced her eyes with a sharp pang. It took her several seconds to get used to the light. She was lying on a hospital bed. A small, old-fashioned TV hung from the wall. To her left was a window with the blinds closed. To her right, a beeping monitor.

Jessica recognized the place. Saint-Mary of all places. She chuckled but was interrupted by a fit of cough. Her lungs burned with every breath.

After a while, the room spinning around her slowly stopped. She bit her lip until she drew blood, afraid of looking down. However, curiosity eventually got the best of her.

Her legs were covered in bandages all the way to her thighs. Her eyes watered as images manifested in her brain without her control. The look on Oliver's face. The fire. The shockwave of the explosion had pushed her back all the way to the end of the hallway. Nothing else after that.

Oliver...

She reached out, her hands patting the sheets until she found a controller to call the nurse. Not even two minutes later, a voluptuous nurse stumbled her way inside.

"You're awake!" she beamed. "Is everything okay, honey?"

"Oliver," Jessica gasped, her throat ached. "Where . . . is he okay?"

The nurse gave her an awkward smile. "Rest for now, sweetie. I'm going to let the doctor know you're awake, and he'll answer all of your questions. Do you need anything else?"

"Water . . ."

The nurse left and hurried back with a cup of water in no time. The doctor arrived soon after. Getting the words out of him was tough. He informed her that her legs had sustained third-degree burns, and it would be a while before she could leave the hospital.

There goes my bikini body, she thought bitterly while the doctor rambled on about how important it was to treat the skin even after leaving the hospital. She dozed off during most of the conversation, though. Her mind was focused on Oliver and Freddy and all the events that had transpired. The doctor didn't seem to know much about the situation, only that she came there with severe burns and needed immediate treatment.

After the doctor left, she decided to turn on the TV. After all, gazing up at the ceiling had gotten old quickly. The news channel was the first thing on. She sat up with difficulty. The news reporter informed about the murder of Timothy Wilson after a break-in in his penthouse. The young CEO had a prominent career ahead and had planned to take a trip with his family until a robber entered and assaulted the family. Timothy had died protecting his wife and kids.

Jessica had a hard time hearing it. She was tempted to turn off the TV right then and there. But she sat through it, barely managing not to tear up in the process. And, of course, the death of Timothy Wilson was the most prominent first news report, considering how big of a figure Timothy had been.

The second report was about a body found in a residence from a local, up-and-coming neighborhood. One of the neighbors discovered it, a sweet-looking old lady who seemed mortified by the event. She went on to tell how she found a severed hand in the freezer. The channel then proceeded to show a picture of the owner of the house, Matthew Walker, who was the prime suspect of the murders. Later that same day, however, his body was found split in half by a chainsaw in an abandoned meat processing factory.

Jessica felt her stomach turn. As horrific as the image was, she felt no regret whatsoever for what she'd done. Even if she would never be able to sleep again after sawing a man in half, it was worth it if it meant ridding the world of a man like that.

A monster, there was no other word for it.

The body of a man dressed in a clown costume had also been found mangled in between the rails of the rollercoaster of a nearby fair. The police declared that the murders did not seem to have any relation to each other.

Jessica sighed in relief. In between reports, she had learned that Jackie had managed to get rid of the uniform that Jessica had "borrowed" and swap it for the hoodie and jeans she was wearing before. Jessica didn't hear another word from Jackie but figured Jackie would stay quiet about their encounter, considering how Jessica didn't hear a single word from her.

Next came the suicide of Roger Johnson. That one was also hard to watch, but Jessica had to know that she was clear of any links to any of those events. The information was brief and to the point, which made her question just how much the reporters and the police knew.

A car had been found sunk in the river with the body of an unidentified man. Jessica shivered as she knew that Stephen was never going to be a problem anymore. As grim as that thought was, the truth was that she felt as if a huge burden had been taken off her shoulders.

And then the last news report of the night came, and it was the hardest one to watch.

The reporter spoke about the explosion in a residency that had taken the lives of two young men, twenty-six-year-old Oliver Grant and nineteen-year-old Freddy Grant.

Jessica had cried all night, unable to fall asleep. The only thing left to do was to let out all of her sorrows and pain as best she could.

The police came the next morning and interrogated her regarding the "incident" in Oliver's house. She could feel her heart pounding in her throat the entire time, but she had managed to keep her poker face.

She declared that Oliver was an old friend and that she had been visiting him when the computer in his cousin's room malfunctioned.

They concluded that a leak in one of the oxygen tanks, along with the spark from a nearby outlet, was what caused the explosion.

Jessica figured it was for the best that the Grant family didn't know the full, ugly truth.

The police did not ask her anything related to the other incidents. They didn't seem to have linked the events together, at least not yet. And by the time they did, if they ever did, she'd be long gone to start a new life. Not out of fear, she was tired of living her life in fear. It was the freedom she sought. The ghosts of her past would not shackle her anymore. She was now ready to hit the reset button and accomplish what she had set up for her life. What grew inside her heart was no longer this ominous feeling of uncertainty. It was hope.

WOULD YOU LIKE TO LEAVE A REVIEW?

As an author, I highly appreciate the feedback I get from my readers. Reviews also help others to make an informed decision before buying. If you enjoyed this book, please consider leaving a short review.

Made in the USA
Coppell, TX
08 November 2022